THE LEMUR

THE LEMUR

BENJAMIN BLACK

ISIS

LARGE PRINT

Oxford

Copyright © Benjamin Black, 2008

First published in Great Britain 2008
by
Picador
an imprint of
Pan Macmillan Ltd.

Published in Large Print 2009 by ISIS Publishing Ltd.,
7 Centremead, Osney Mead, Oxford OX2 0ES
by arrangement with
Pan Macmillan Ltd.

British Library Cataloguing in Publication Data
Black, Benjamin, 1945–
    The Lemur. – Large print ed.
    1. Irish Americans – Fiction
    2. Billionaires – Fiction
    3. Authors – Fiction
    4. Extortion – Fiction
    5. Murder – Fiction
    6. Suspense fiction
    7. Large type books
    I. Title
    823.9'2 [F]

ISBN 978–0–7531–8272–7 (hb)
ISBN 978–0–7531–8273–4 (pb)

Printed and bound in Great Britain by
T. J. International Ltd., Padstow, Cornwall

CHAPTER
ONE

Glass Houses

The researcher was a very tall, very thin young man with a head too small for his frame and an adam's apple the size of a golf ball. He wore rimless spectacles, the lenses of which were almost invisible, the shine of the glass giving an extra lustre to his large, round, slightly bulging black eyes. A spur of blond hair sprouted from his chin, and his brow, high and domed, was pitted with acne scars. His hands were slender and pearly-pale, with long, tapering fingers — a girl's hands, or at least the hands a girl should have. Even though he was sitting down, the crotch of his baggy jeans sagged halfway to his knees. His none-too-clean tee-shirt bore the legend *Life Sucks And Then You Die*. He looked about seventeen but must be, John Glass guessed, in his late twenties, at least. With that long neck and little head and those big, shiny eyes, he bore a strong resemblance to one of the more exotic rodents, though for the moment Glass could not think which one.

His name was Dylan Riley. Of course, Glass thought, he would be a Dylan.

"So," Riley said, "you're married to Big Bill's daughter."

He was lounging in a black-leather swivel chair in Glass's borrowed office on the north-facing side of Mulholland Tower. Behind him, through a wall of plate-glass, grey Manhattan sulked steamily under a drifting pall of April rain.

"Does that seem funny to you?" Glass enquired. He had an instinctive dislike of people who wore tee-shirts with smart things written on them.

Dylan Riley snickered. "Not funny, no. Surprising. I wouldn't have picked you as one of Big Bill's people."

Glass decided to let that go. He had begun to breathe heavily through his nostrils, *hiss*-hiss, *hiss*-hiss, always a warning sign.

"*Mister* Mulholland," Glass said heavily, "is eager that I have all the facts, and that I have them the right way round."

Riley smiled his goofy smile and swivelled the chair first to one side and then the other, nodding happily. "All the facts," he said, "sure." He seemed to be enjoying himself.

"Yes," Glass said, with stony emphasis, "all the facts. That's why I'm hiring you."

In one corner of the office there was a big square metal desk, and Glass went now and sat down carefully behind it. He felt less panic-stricken sitting down. The office was on the thirty-ninth floor. It was absurd to be expected to conduct business — to do anything — at such a height. On his first day there he had edged up to the plate-glass wall and peered down to see, a couple of floors below, fluffy white clouds that looked like soft icebergs sailing sedately across a submerged city. Now he put his hands flat on the desk before him as if it were a raft he was trying to hold steady. He very much needed a cigarette.

Dylan Riley had turned the chair round to face the desk. Glass was sure the young man could sense how dizzy and sick he felt, perched up here in this crystal-and-steel eyrie.

"Anyway," Glass said, moving his right hand in a wide are across the desktop as if to sweep the subject aside; the gesture made him think of footage of Richard Nixon, sweating on the evening news all those years ago, insisting he was not a crook. The studios were so harshly lit in those days of paranoia and recrimination they had made pretty well everyone look like a villain in an old Eastman Color movie. "I should tell you," Glass said, "that Mr Mulholland will give you no assistance. And I don't want you to approach him. Don't call, don't write. Understand?"

Riley bit his lower lip, which made him look all the more like — what was it? A squirrel? No. Close, but no. "You haven't told him," Riley said, "have you? About me, I mean."

Glass ignored that. "I'm not asking you to be a muck-raker," he said. "I don't expect Mr Mulholland to have guilty secrets. He was an undercover agent, but he's not a crook, in case you think I think he is."

"No," Riley said, "he's your father-in-law."

Glass was breathing heavily again. "That's something I'd like you to forget about," he said, "when you come to do your researches." He sat back on his chair and studied the young man. "How will you go about it — researching, I mean?"

Riley laced his long pale fingers over his concave stomach and this time rocked himself gently backwards and forwards in the swivel chair, making the ball-and-socket mechanism underneath the seat squeal tinily, *eek, eek*.

"Well," Riley said, "let's say I go way beyond Wikipedia."

"But you'll use . . . computers, and so on?" Glass did not possess even a mobile phone.

"Oh, yes, computers," Riley said, making his big eyes bigger still, mocking the older man, "all sorts of wizard gadgets, don't you know."

Glass wondered if that was supposed to be a British accent. Did Riley think he was English? Well, let him.

He imagined lighting up: the match flaring, the lovely tang of sulphur, and then the harsh smoke searing his throat.

"I want to ask you something," Riley said, thrusting his pin-head forward on its tall stalk of neck. "Why did you agree to it?"

"What?"

"To write Big Bill's biography."

"I don't think that's any of your business," Glass said sharply. He looked out at the misty rain. He had moved permanently from Dublin to New York six months previously, he had an apartment on Central Park West and a house on Long Island — or at least his wife had — yet he had still not got used to what he thought of as the New York Jeer. The fellow on the street corner selling you a hotdog would say, "Thanks, bud," and manage to make it sound merrily derisive. How did they keep it going, this endless, amused, argumentative squaring up to each other and everyone else?

"Tell me," he said, "what you know about Mr Mulholland."

"For free?" Riley grinned again, then leaned back and looked at the ceiling, fingering the tuft of hair on his chin. "William 'Big Bill' Mulholland. South Boston Irish, second generation. Father ran off when wee Willie was a kid, mother took in laundry, scrubbed floors. In school William got straight As, impressed the priests, was an altar boy, the usual. Tough, though — any paedophile cleric coming near Bill Mulholland would likely have lost his balls. Put himself through Boston College. Engineering. At college was recruited into the CIA, became a working operative late forties. Electronic surveillance was his specialty. Korea, Latin America, Europe, Vietnam. Then he had a run-in with James Jesus Angleton over Angleton's obsessive distrust of the French — Big Bill was posted to the Company's Paris bureau at the time. In those days one did not incur the displeasure" — again that hopeless attempt at a British accent — "of James Jesus without getting cut off at the knees, which is what would have happened to Bill Mulholland if he hadn't got out before Angleton could give him the shove, or worse. That was the late sixties."

He pushed himself up out of the chair, unwinding himself like a fakir's rope, and shambled to the glass wall and stood looking out, his hands thrust into the back pockets of his jeans. He went on: "After he left the Company Big Bill got into the then blossoming communications business, where he put his training as a spook to good use when he set up Mulholland Cable and right away began to make shitloads of money. It wasn't until twenty years later that he had to bring in his *protégé* Charlie Varriker to save the firm from going bust." He paused, and without turning said: "You'll know about Big Bill's matrimonial adventures, I guess? In 1949 he married the world's most famous redhead, Vanessa Lane, Hollywood actress, if that's the word, and in 1949 the marriage was duly dissolved." Now he grinned over his shoulder at Glass. "Ain't love just screwy?"

He went back to contemplating the misted city and was silent for a moment, thinking. "You know," he said, "he's such a CIA cliché I wonder if the CIA didn't invent him. Look at his next marriage, in 'fifty-eight, to Claire Thorpington Eliot, of the Boston Eliots — that was some step up the social ladder for Billy the Kid from Brewster Street. He had, as you will know, one child only, a daughter, Louise, by the second Mrs Mulholland. Miz Claire, as this grand lady was called, died in a hunting accident — balking horse, broken neck — in April 1961, on the eve, as bloody-minded Fate would have it, of the invasion of the Playa Girón, otherwise known as the Bay of Pigs, a venture in which Big Bill was sunk up to his neck. The grieving widower returned from the shores of Florida to find the Eliots already moving his things, including his two-year-old daughter, out of the grand old family mansion in Back Bay."

He turned and walked back and slumped down in the chair and again turned his eyes to the ceiling. "Next thing," he said, "Big Bill was married a third time, to Nancy Harrison, writer, journalist and Martha Gellhorn lookalike, and living with her on a fine estate in County Somewhere on the west coast of Ireland, not an Oscar statuette's throw from the home of his old friend and drinking buddy John Huston. Grand days, by all accounts, but bound to end, like all such. Blonde Nancy couldn't take the endless rain and the low-browed natives, and packed up her Remington and high-tailed it for sunnier climes — Ibiza, Clifford Irving, Orson Welles, all that." He stopped, and lowered his glossy gaze from the ceiling and fixed on Glass. "You want more, I got more. And I haven't even looked into the crystal ball of my laptop yet."

"What did you do?" Glass said. "Learn this stuff off before you came up here?"

A sharp something came into the young man's look, a resentful edge. "I have a photographic memory."

"Useful, in your trade," Glass said.

"Yeah."

He was, Glass saw, sulking. His professional honour had been questioned. It was good to know where he was vulnerable.

Glass rose, a finger braced against the desktop for balance, and launched himself cautiously out into the room. At each step he took he felt he was about to fall over, and had the impression that he was yawing

7

sideways irresistibly in the direction of the glass wall and the gulp-inducing nothingness beyond. Would he ever become accustomed to this cloud-capped tower?

"I can see," he said, "I've picked the right person. Because what I want is detail — the kind of thing I'm not going to have the time to find for myself, or the inclination, frankly."

"No," Riley said, from the leather depths of his chair, still sounding surly, "detail was never your strong point, was it?"

What struck Glass was not so much the implied insult as the tense in which it was couched. Was this how everyone would see it, that by agreeing to write his father-in-law's biography he had renounced his calling as a journalist? If so, they would be wrong, though once again it was a matter of tense. For he had already given up journalism, before ever Big Bill had approached him with an offer it would have been foolish to refuse. His reports on Northern Ireland during the Troubles, on the massacre in Tiananmen Square, on the Rwandan genocide, on the Intifada, on that bloody Saturday afternoon in Srebrenica, not so much reports as extended and passionately fashioned jeremiads — there would be no more of them. Something had ceased in him, a light had been extinguished, he did not know why. It was simply that: he had burned out. An old story. He was a walking cliché. "I want you to write this thing, son," Big Bill had said to him, laying a hand on his shoulder, "not only because I trust you, but because others do, too. I don't want a hagiography — I don't merit one, I'm no saint. What I want is the truth." And Glass had thought: Ah, the truth.

"It's not going to be easy for you," he said now to the young man lounging in the shell-shaped chair.

"How's that?"

"I don't want Mr Mulholland to come to hear of you and what you're doing. You understand?"

He turned — too quickly, making his head spin — and gave Dylan Riley what he hoped was a hard look. But Riley was gazing at the ceiling again, gnawing the nail of his left little finger, and might not have been listening.

"That's my job," Riley said, "to be discreet. Anyway, you'd be surprised how much information — detail, as you say — is on record, if you know where to look for it."

Glass suddenly wanted to be rid of the fellow. "Have you a standard contract?" he asked brusquely.

"A contract? I don't do contracts." Riley smiled slyly. "I trust you."

"Oh, yes? I didn't think you'd trust anyone, given the nature of your work."

Riley stood up from the chair and adjusted the crotch of his sagging jeans with scooping gestures of both hands. He really was an unappetising person. "The nature of my work?" he said. "I'm a researcher, Mr Glass. That's all."

"Yes, but you find things out, and surely sometimes the things you find out are not to the taste of your employers, never mind the people they are having researched."

Riley gave him a long, piercing look, putting his head on one side and narrowing his eyes. "You said Big Bill has no guilty secrets."

"I said I expect none."

"I'm here to tell you everybody has secrets, mostly guilty ones."

Glass turned towards the door, drawing the young man with him. "You'll get to work straight away," he said, a statement not a question. "When can I expect to hear from you?"

"I've got to get my head round this, get organised, decide priorities. Then we'll talk again." By now Glass had the door open. The much-used air in the corridor smelled faintly of burned rubber. "I've got to get my head around *you*, too," Riley said, with a suddenly bitter laugh. "I used to read you, you know, in the *Guardian*, in *Rolling Stone*, the *New York Review*. And now you're writing Big Bill Mulholland's life story." He inflated his cheeks and released the air in them with a tiny, plosive sound. "Wow," he said, and turned away.

Glass shut the door and walked back to his desk, and when he reached it, as if at a signal, the telephone rang. "This is Security, Mr Glass. Your wife is here."

For a moment Glass said nothing. He touched the chair Dylan Riley had sat in, and again it made its tiny protest: *eek, eek*. The young man had left a definite odour on the air, a greyish, rank spoor.

A lemur! That was the creature Dylan Riley resembled. Yes, of course. A lemur.

"Tell her to come up," John Glass said.

CHAPTER
TWO

Louise

Louise Glass was forty-eight and looked thirty. She was tall and slim and a redhead, though these days most of the red came out of a bottle. Her skin was pale to the point of translucency, and her sharp-featured face was lovely from some angles and fascinatingly harsh from others. She was, Glass acknowledged to himself, for the umpteenth time, a magnificent woman, and he no longer loved her. It was strange. One day, around the time he had given up being a journalist, all that he had felt for her, all that helpless, half-tormented passion, had dropped to degree zero. It was as if the flesh-and-blood woman had, like an enchanted princess in a fairy tale, been turned to stone in his arms. There she was, as she had always been, a smooth, svelte, burnished beauty, at the mere sight of whom in former days something in him would cry out piteously, in a kind of happy anguish, but whose presence now provoked in him only a faint, fading melancholy.

Today she wore a dark-green suit and a Philip Treacy hat that was a minuscule square of black velvet topped with a few wisps of what might be spun sugar.

"What's the matter?" she asked. "You look ghastly."

"It's this place."

She looked about the office, frowning. It was she who had suggested he borrow the room — her father owned the building. "What's wrong with it?"

He did not want to admit his fright at being almost forty floors above street level. "It's too impersonal. I don't know if I can write here."

"You could work at the apartment."

"You know I can't write at home."

She settled on him her grey-green gaze. "*Is* it home?" The silence that followed this was a chasm into which they both cast a glance and then stepped quickly back.

"You could go out to Silver Barn." Silver Barn was their — her — house on Long Island. "The study is all set up. It's quiet, no one to disturb you." He pulled a face. "Well then," she said, with a tightening of the lips, "if you can't work, you can take me to lunch."

They walked east along Forty-fourth Street and Glass at last got to smoke a cigarette. The fine rain drifted down absent-mindedly, like ectoplasm. The trouble with smoking was that the desire to smoke was so much greater than the satisfaction afforded by actually smoking. Sometimes when he had a cigarette going he would forget and reach for the packet and start to light another. Maybe that was the thing to do, smoke six at a time, three in the gaps between the fingers of each hand, achieve a Gatling-gun effect.

Mario's was crowded, as usual these days. The red-check tablecloths and rickety bentwood chairs proclaimed a peasant plainness that was contradicted by the breathtaking prices on the menu. The Glasses had been coming here since the early days of the establishment, long before they had moved permanently to New York, when Mario himself was still in charge and the place really was plain. They had nicknamed it the Bleeding Horse, for reasons no longer remembered. Now Louise gave up her dripping umbrella to a waiter and they were shown to their usual table in a corner by the window, set, Glass noted, for three. Flutes of Prosecco were brought at once. "I wish," Louise murmured, "I had the courage to tell them what a common drink I think this is."

Glass said nothing. He liked Prosecco. He liked the gesture, too, the drinks coming uncalled-for and set down before them with an actorly flourish. It made him feel an old New York hand; he could almost see the caption, *Glass in the Bleeding Horse, one of his favourite Manhattan eateries*. He often thought of his life in journalese; it was an old habit. He wondered if Louise considered him common, too, like the wine.

"How *is* the work?" his wife asked, her eyes on the menu. "Have you made a start yet?" The rain-light from the window gave her the look of an early Florentine madonna, as she sat there with her long, angular, pale face inclined, and the menu she was holding might have been a psalter.

"No," he said, "I haven't made a start. I mean, I haven't started writing. There are things I have to do first."

"Research, you mean?"

He looked at her sharply. But there was no way she could know about Dylan Riley; he had told no one about the Lemur. She was still reading the menu, bringing to it the rapt, radiant attention that she brought to everything she did, even, he ruefully recalled, lovemaking.

"Yes, research," he mumbled, "that kind of thing."

The waiter came and Glass ordered linguine with clams and Louise asked for a plain green salad. It was all she ever ate at lunchtime. Why then, Glass wondered, did she spend so long poring over the menu? Having taken their order, the waiter pointed his pencil enquiringly at the empty third place, but Louise shook her head. "David might look in," she told Glass. "I said we'd eat and he could join us for coffee."

Glass made no comment. David Sinclair was Louise's son by her first marriage, to a Wall Street lawyer who seemed to have passed through her life leaving hardly a trace, except, of course, the young man who now occupied the centre of her world. Glass looked round for the waiter and the wine list; if his stepson was joining them he would need more than a glass of Prosecco.

Their food arrived and they ate in silence for a time. The small rain wept against the window-pane and the cars and taxis going past shimmered and slid as in a wet mirage. Glass was wondering why he felt the need to be so secretive about Dylan Riley. Bill Mulholland's life was emblematic of the last two-thirds of the chaotic, violent and dizzyingly innovative century that had ended not so long ago. No one would expect a biographer to do unaided the extensive research that would be required for the writing of the life of such

14

a man — no one, except that man himself. Bill Mulholland was the original rugged individualist and required those around him to be made of the same stern stuff. What sort of sissy writer would hire someone else to do the donkey work? He had offered the commission, along with a million-dollar fee, to his son-in-law because, as he had said, he trusted him; trusted him, that is, as Glass well understood, to leave certain, overly heavy stones unturned. It was Glass himself — not his father-in-law, as he had told Dylan Riley — who wanted all the facts, even, or especially, the inconvenient ones. Glass believed Aristotle was right: he that holds a secret holds power.

He took a drink of wine and studied his wife. She was attending to her plate of greens with the longnecked, finical concentration of a heron at the water's edge. She had urged him strongly to accept her father's offer. "You used to like nothing better than a challenge," she had said, "and writing my father's life will be nothing if not that." He had noted then, too, the tense employed. *Used to.* "And a million dollars," she had added, with a lopsided, ironical smile, "is a million dollars."

It was not the money that had made him take on the job. What, then? He supposed Louise was right. What greater challenge could there be than to write the official biography of his own father-in-law, one of the fiercest and most controversial of that last cohort of Cold Warriors who had, so they believed, brought the Evil Empire to the dust?

"You know you'll have to give the manuscript to the boys at Langley for their okay," his father-in-law had told him, with that famous twinkle. "There are some things that can never get told." And Glass, remembering that remark, thought again now of Nixon, poor old Tricky Dick, sweating under the arc lamps, in another age.

David Sinclair arrived. He was tall and sleekly slim, like his mother, but black-haired and swarthy where she was russet and pearl — Rubin Sinclair, his father, was a hirsute and barely civilised redneck from Kentucky. David was handsome, in a dandyish sort of way, but his slightly protruding eyes were set unfortunately close together — whenever Glass contemplated his stepson he recalled Truman Capote saying of Marlene Dietrich that if her eyes had been a fraction nearer to each other she would have been a chicken. Waspish, wicked Truman. Glass had tried to interview him once, over a hopelessly bibulous lunch at the Four Seasons in the middle of which the sozzled novelist had laid his cheek on the tablecloth and gone noisily to sleep. Glass at the time was young enough not to be embarrassed, and contentedly finished his broiled squab and the remains of a bottle of Mouton Rothschild, calm in the knowledge that the lavish treat was being paid for by the *Sunday Times* of London.

"Hello," David Sinclair said to Glass, sliding sinuously into his seat and unfolding a napkin across his lap. His attitude always towards his stepfather was one of amused scepticism. "How is the great world?"

Glass smiled thinly. "It wasn't so great," he said, "the last time I looked."

David ordered peppermint tea. He was dressed in a dark-wool suit and a white silk shirt and silk tie. His watch was a Patek Philippe, one of the more discreet models. His mother pampered him; he was her weakness.

"David has some news for you," she said now. "Haven't you, darling?"

The young man raised his eyebrows and briefly closed his eyes, his version of a shrug. "I thought you would have told him yourself by now, you're so excited about it," he said.

Louise turned to her husband. "David is joining the foundation."

He looked at her blankly. "The foundation?"

"For goodness' sake, John! The Mulholland Trust. In fact, he's going to be the new director."

"Oh."

"Is that all you can say — *oh*?"

"I thought *you* were the director."

"I was. It was becoming too much for me, I told you that. From now on I'll take a back seat."

"Isn't he" — Glass took a small pleasure in speaking pointedly of his stepson as if he were not there — "isn't he a little young to take on so great a responsibility?"

David laughed shortly, for some reason of his own, and sipped his tea.

"I'll still be there, to help him, at first," Louise said. She always resented being required to explain herself.

17

"Besides, there's the staff. They're all experienced people."

Glass contemplated the young man sitting with his back to the window and smirking. "Well," he said, lifting his wine glass, "congratulations, young man." He tended not to address his stepson by name, if he could help it.

"Thanks, *Dad*," David said, with high sarcasm, and lifted his teacup to return the toast.

Suddenly Glass remembered the first time he and Louise had met, one April afternoon at John Huston's mansion near Loughrea in the wet and stormy west of Ireland. He had been a precocious nineteen, and had come to interview the film director for the *Irish Times*. Bill Mulholland and his daughter were there. They had ridden over from the mansion down the valley that Mulholland had recently purchased, and Louise wore stained jodhpurs and a green silk scarf knotted at her throat. She was barely seventeen. Her skin was flushed pink from the ride, and there was a sprinkling of freckles on the bridge of her perfect nose, and Glass could hardly speak from the effort of trying not to stare at her. Huston, the old satyr, saw at a glance what was going on in the young man's breast, and grinned his orang-utan's grin and handed him a dry martini and said: "Here, son, have a bracer."

David Sinclair had finished his tea and now he rose, shooting his cuffs. He had to be somewhere, he said smoothly, giving the impression that it was somewhere much too important for its name to be spoken aloud in public. Glass saw how pleased with himself he was.

Director of the Mulholland Trust at the age of — what was he? — twenty-three? Young enough, Glass thought with satisfaction, to make a serious mess of it. His mother, of course, would shield him from the worst of his mistakes, but Big Bill, the founder of the Trust, was not as fond of his grandson as Louise would wish him to be, and Big Bill was not a great forgiver.

When the young man had gone Louise signalled for the check and turned to her husband and said: "I wonder if you realise how clearly you betray your jealousy."

Glass stared. "Who am I jealous of?"

She handed her platinum credit card to the waiter, who went away and came back in a moment with the receipt. She signed her fine, firm signature and he gave her the copy and departed. Glass watched as she folded the receipt carefully four times lengthwise and then slipped the spill she had made into her purse. That was Louise's way: fold and file, fold and file. "I'm surprised Amex haven't done a card specially for you," Glass said mildly. "In Kryptonite, perhaps." She ignored this; his barbed jokes she always ignored. She looked down at the tablecloth, fingering the weave of it. "The Trust does valuable work, you know," she said, "more than valuable, not least in helping to resolve that late, nasty little conflict in your native land."

He marvelled always at the way she spoke, in moulded sentences, with such preciseness, making such nice discriminations; her three years of study in England, a postgraduate course among the Oxford logical positivists, had honed her diction to a gleaming keenness.

"I know," he said, trying not to sound petulant, "I know what the Trust does."

She brushed his protest aside. "You, of course, are too cynical and, yes, too jealous to acknowledge the importance of what we do. Frankly, I don't care. I long ago stopped caring what you think or don't think. But I won't have you trying to infect my son with your bitterness. Your failures are not his fault — they're no one's fault but your own. So keep your sarcasm to yourself." She lifted her eyes from the tablecloth and looked at him. Her gaze was as blank as the face of her son's expensive watch, with a myriad unseen, infinitely intricate movements going on behind it. "Do you understand?"

"I'm going out to smoke a cigarette," he said.

The rain had stopped and the street was steaming under watery sunlight. He walked back to the office, the chill of early spring striking at him through the light stuff of his jacket. He was thinking of Dylan Riley, picturing him in some Village loft hunched over his machines, the screens throwing their nocturnal radiance on to his face and printing their images on the shiny dark ovals of his eyes. It was to be a week before Glass would hear from him again, and then he would learn how sharp and penetrating was the Lemur's bite.

CHAPTER
THREE

The Bite

Glass had spent the week in his office, trying his best to get used to it, to the plate glass and the steel, to the deadened air, to, above all, the heady elevation. He tried to keep office hours, breezing in at nine but slouching out again morosely five or six hours later. One day, when it occurred to him that there was no one to challenge him, he smoked a cigarette, leaning back luxuriously on his chair with his feet on the desk and his ankles crossed. No forbidden cigarette ever, including the ones he used to pilfer from his father's coat pocket when he was a ten-year-old, had tasted so sweet, so dangerous, so sexy.

Presently, however, he saw the problems he had given himself. How was he to get rid of the smell of smoke, since the windows up here were sealed tight? The telltale stink would probably cling for weeks in this endlessly recycled air. And in the more immediate term, what was he to do with the ash or — Jesus! — with the stub? In the end he fashioned a makeshift ashtray from the foil of a Hershey bar wrapper that someone had left in the wastepaper basket, feeling as proudly resourceful and inventive as Robinson Crusoe.

When he was finished he folded the wrapper as neatly as Louise would have done and put it into his pocket — surprising how much heat had been left in the stubbed-out butt — and crept with a felon's circumspection to the men's room and locked himself in a stall and emptied the contents of the foil into the lavatory bowl. But of course the filter tip was too buoyant to go down — even some of the ash stayed on the surface of the water — and in the end, after repeated vain flushings, he had to fish the soggy thing out and wrap it in a wad of toilet tissue and carry it back to the office and throw it into the waste bin where, he gloomily supposed, some cleaner or busybody janitor would nose it out and denounce him.

What about real addicts, he wondered, poor wretches hooked on heroin or crack cocaine — or that new stuff, something meth? Were their lives a series of grimly comic frustrations and inept subterfuges? He supposed they must be, though he supposed too that junkies would not see the funny side of things. Not that he was laughing, exactly.

The laptop computer that Mulholland's people had supplied him with, sleek, gleaming, gunmetal-grey, sat before him on the desk, daring him to open it. So far he had passed up the dare. He was a long way from being ready to start writing — oh, a long, long way, weeks, at least, maybe months. He spent the empty hours of his working days browsing through histories of the OSS and the CIA and the FBI, the DST and the DGSE and the SDECE, the NKVD and the KGB and the GRU — the Soviets were whimsically prone to change the names of their security agencies — and, of course, MI5 and MI6, the difference between which he could never keep clear in his mind. Stumbling about in this bristling thicket of acronyms he felt like the dull but honest hero of a cautionary folktale, who must make his way through a maze of magical signs and indecipherable portents to the lair of the great wizard.

And there *was* something of the magus about Big Bill Mulholland. He had been, or claimed to have been, that rarest of birds among a teeming aviary of rareties: an agent with a conscience. There were people in what Glass the cliché-hater told himself he must remember not to call the *highest echelons* of the West's intelligence services who swore by Big Bill's probity; there were also those who swore at it. Allen Dulles himself, when he was director of the CIA, had once been heard referring to Big Bill, in an uncharacteristic lapse from his usual urbanity, as "that goddamned sanctimonious son of a bitch". For William Mulholland, whose second name was, with awful aptness, Pius, was seized of the lifelong conviction that even, or perhaps especially, the intelligence services had a duty to be as frank and open with the public as the dictates of security would allow. "Otherwise," as he so simply put it, "why call ourselves a democracy?" And this doctrine, Glass often reminded himself, had been laid down *in the nineteen fifties*, and the *early* nineteen fifties, at that, when Joe McCarthy and his crew were still cocks of the anti-Red walk. Big Bill attributed his compulsive honesty to the influence of his beloved mother, Margaret Mary Mulholland, of blessèd memory. She would probably, would Margaret Mary, require an entire chapter of her son's biography, John Glass had glumly to acknowledge. He would earn that million bucks.

When the telephone rang it made him jump. He secretly hated telephones, for they frightened him. It was, he noted by the baleful clock that glowered at him from the wall opposite his desk, 10.47a.m. The day was bright but windy, and since his arrival he had been trying not to notice the way the entire building quivered almost voluptuously under the strokings of the stronger gusts.

"Hi there," the voice said, and although Glass had been waiting all week for this call, for a moment he did not recognise the voice. There was a soft laugh on the line. "Riley here. Your hired bloodhound, don't you know." It occurred to Glass that perhaps the fellow was not parodying his accent after all, and that the plummy tone he liked to put on was meant to make him sound like Sherlock Holmes, or Lord Peter Wimsey.

"I wondered where you'd got to," Glass said.

"Well, I got to all sorts of places, virtually and otherwise. And turned up all sorts of things."

Glass had an image of some gawky bird under a bush probing and pecking among a mulch of dead leaves. "Oh?" he said.

"*Owh*," Riley echoed, and this time there was no doubt that he was mimicking Glass's way of speaking. "*Owh* is right." There was a silence. Glass did not know what to say, what prompt to supply. A faint, a very faint, niggle of unease had set itself up in the region of

24

his diaphragm. "Listen," Riley said, and Glass had a distinct impression of the young man leisurely stretching back in a chair and clawing absently at the roomy crotch of his jeans, "for a start I know what Big Bill is paying you to write up his colourful life-story."

Glass heard himself swallow. He had thought that he and his wife and his father-in-law were the only ones who knew that figure. How could the Lemur have found it out? Big Bill would surely be the last one to blab that kind of thing. Had Louise been talking? Not like her, either. "I'm sure," Glass said measuredly, "you'll have got hold of a wildly exaggerated sum."

The Lemur did not bother insisting. "We didn't discuss my fee," he said.

"I asked if you had a standard contract — remember?"

"The point is, this is turning out not to be a standard job."

Glass waited, but the young man was in no hurry; it was apparent even down the phone line that he was once again enjoying himself. "Come on," Glass said, trying to sound unconcerned, "tell me what it is you've stumbled on."

The Lemur did his breathy little laugh. "The way I see it, we're partners in this project — thrown together by chance and the word of whoever it was recommended me to you, but partners all the same. Yes?"

"No. I hired you. I am your employer. You are my employee."

"And given that we find ourselves together in this deal, I think it only fair that I should be an equal partner."

"Meaning?"

"Meaning half a million dollars. Fifty per cent of your fee for writing this hard-hitting and entirely unbiased book. Share and share alike — right, John?"

Glass's upper lip was misted with sweat. His mind went temporarily numb. "Tell me," he said, and it sounded in his ears like a croak, "tell me what you've found out."

Again along the wires there was that sense of luxurious stretching, of pleasurable scratching. "No," Dylan Riley said, "not yet."

"Why?"

There was a pause for thought, then: "I don't know. I guess it's kind of an occupational thing. I learn a secret, I want to hold on to it for a while, roll it around, you know, like good wine on the palate. Does that make sense, old boy?"

A flash of light from outside, extraordinarily bright, burst on Glass's retinas, making him turn his face aside. Had someone in one of the surrounding towers managed to open a window? He peered, but could see no movement out there, no lifted arm or angled pane. He floundered, trying to think what to say next. How had this thing gone wrong, so quickly, so comprehensively? One minute his problem was how to get rid of a cigarette end, the next he was in a sweat while the pinhead he had been foolish enough to hire was trying to blackmail him for half a million dollars. Where was the link, the swaying rope-bridge, between that *then* and this *now*? He put a hand to his forehead; he could hear himself breathing against the mouthpiece of the phone, *hiss*-hiss, *hiss*-hiss.

"Look, Riley —" he began, but was not allowed to go on, which was just as well since he did not know what he was going to say.

"No, you look," the Lemur said, in a new, harsh and suddenly unadolescent-sounding voice. "You used to be the real thing, Glass. A lot of us believed in you, followed your example. Now look at you." He gave a snort of disgust. "Well, sell out to your father-in-law the spook if you like. Tell the world what a sterling guy he is, the unacknowledged Cold War conscience of the West, the man who urged negotiations with Castro and a safe passage for Allende to Russia — as if he'd have wanted to go, the poor schmuck. Go ahead, write his testament, and peddle your soul for a mess of dollars. But I know something that will tear you people apart, and I think you should pay me, I think you *will* pay me, to keep it all in the family." Glass tried to speak but again was silenced. "And want me to tell you something else? I think you know what I know. I think you know very well what I'm talking about, the one thing big enough to screw up the cosy little civilised arrangement you all have going between you. Am I right?"

"I swear," Glass said, more a gasp than a croak this time, "I swear I have no idea what you can have found out."

"Right." Now he was nodding that long narrow head of his. Glass could see it clearly in his mind, the lips pursing up, the little blond goatee wobbling, those startling eyes furiously agleam. "Right. The next call you get about this won't be from me."

The line went dead.

That day thirty years before when Glass and Louise had first met at John Huston's house, St Clerans, in Connemara, the director had taken him for a walk after lunch. By then Big Bill and his daughter had left — the Atlantic wind was still in her hair, Glass caught the coolness of it when she passed him by going out — and Glass too was anxious to be on his way, for he had a deadline to meet. But Huston had insisted on them taking what he called "a tramp" together. He went away and came back half an hour later — Glass had filled the time listening back over the material he had taped — wearing tweed plus-fours and a tweed jacket with a half-belt at the back, and plaid wool socks and walking boots and a floppy peaked cap reminiscent of a cow-pat. He looked as if he had been dressed by a drunk in the costume department for a leading role in *Brigadoon*. He caught Glass's incredulous glance and smiled broadly, showing off his big yellow tombstone teeth, and said: "What do you think, would I pass for a native?" Glass did not know if he should laugh.

They had walked along a boreen and down into the valley. Sunlight and shadow swept the dark-green hillsides, and the birds were whistling madly in the thorn trees, and there was the sound of unseen waters rushing under the heather, and the gorse blossom was already aflame. Huston had lately finished filming *The Man Who Would Be King* and was in reflective mood.

"Who'd have thought," he said, "a Missouri boy would end up here, owning a chunk of the most beautiful country God ever made? I love this place. I've been an Irish citizen since 'sixty-four. I want my bones to rest here, when the time comes." They arrived at a wooden gate and Huston stopped and leaned an elbow on the top bar and turned to Glass and said: "I've been watching you, son. You get so busy asking questions you forget other people can see you. You're ambitious. I approve of that. You're a little bit ruthless, and I approve of that, too. Only the ruthless succeed. But there's something about you that kind of troubles me — I mean, that would worry me, if you were really my son. I'd be kind of scared thinking of you out there in the big, wide world. Maybe it's that you expect too much of people." He unlatched the gate and they walked on along a path into a dense stand of tall pines, where the light turned brownish-blue and the air was colder somehow than it had been when they were in the open. Huston put an arm round Glass's shoulders and gave him an avuncular squeeze. "Knew a fellow once," he said, "a mobster, one of Meyer Lansky's numbers men. He was a funny guy, I mean witty, you know? I've always remembered something he said to me once. 'If you don't know who the patsy in the room is, it's you.' " Huston gave an emphysemic laugh, the phlegm twanging deep in his chest. "That was Joey Cohen's gift of wisdom to me — 'If you don't know who the patsy is, it's you.' " The director's big, shapely hand closed on Glass's shoulder again. "You should remember it too, son. Joey knew what he was talking about."

Now, in his office teetering high above Forty-fourth Street, Glass held the phone in a hand that refused to stay steady and tapped out a number. A bright New York voice answered, doing its singsong *yes-how-may-I-help-you?*.

"Alison O'Keeffe," Glass said. "Is she there? Tell her it's John — she'll know."

He drummed his fingers on the desk and listened to the hollow nothingness on the line. Can there be, he was thinking, any more costly hostage to fortune than a mistress?

CHAPTER
FOUR

Alison

Glass had first met Alison O'Keeffe the previous winter outside a bar in the Village. It was, *she* was, every middle-aged male smoker's fantasy made flesh. There he stood, huddled in the doorway sucking on a cigarette as flurries of snow played round his ankles, when she came out, scowled at the bruise-coloured sky and lit up a Gauloise — a Gauloise, for God's sake! He assumed from this that she was French, but the longer he looked at her — and he looked at her for so long and with such intensity that he was surprised she did not call a cop — the more convinced he became, on no basis other than tribal instinct, that she must be Irish. She was of middle height, slender, very dark of hair and very pale of skin. The word he could not help applying to her features was "chiselled", though they were far from hard — creamy marble, lovingly shaped. Her eyes were an extraordinary shade of deep azure, which, as he would come to know, grew even deeper at moments of passion. She smoked now in that faintly impatient, faintly resentful way that women did when they were forced outdoors like this, one arm held stiffly upright, an elbow cupped firmly in a palm, her fingers twiddling the cigarette as if it were a piece of chalk with which she was dashing out a complex formula on an invisible blackboard. She wore a high-necked black sweater and black leather trousers; the trousers he considered a mistake, but one that, on balance, he could forgive.

Afterwards he would insist that he was in love with her before they had exchanged their first words.

She paid him no heed, and seemed not to have noticed him there, though they were the only two pariahs in the smokers' vestibule at that five o'clock hour of the darkling December evening. He had come to the bar to meet the editor of a new radical journal who wanted him to contribute a piece on the Northern Irish peace agreement for the first issue. The editor was a muscular, fresh-faced, tirelessly smiling young man recently out of Yale, and after two minutes of his pitch Glass knew he was not going to write for him. That kind of sincerity, though he supposed he, too, must have been filled with it, and filled to the brim, back at the dawn of history, now only wearied him. So he would not have been eager to go back into the bar even if this palely lovely girl had not been outside with him, which she most certainly, most excitingly, was. Well, not with him, perhaps, but there, which for the moment was enough. He wondered how he might go about securing her attention. It was odd how perilous it could be in this city to offer a friendly remark to a stranger. Once he had commented on the weather to a girl in a lift, and she had shrunk back from him into a corner and informed him in a tense, low voice that she had a Mace spray in her purse. This one irritably smoking beside him now, in her shiny rawhide pants, looked as if she would be not so antagonistic, though her self-containedness was certainly daunting. But it was Christmas, the time of year most fraught, for him, with erotic possibilities, and he had a panicky sense that at the very next moment this particular possibility was going to stub out her cigarette and thrust herself back into the crowded bar, and that he would never see her again, and so, at last, he spoke.

"I've made a bet with myself," he said.

The young woman looked at him, and seemed not impressed by what she saw. "Pardon me?"

"I'm wagering you're Irish." He smiled; it felt, from his side of it, like a leer.

She narrowed her eyes and set her jaw at an angle, weighing him up. "How did you know?" she said.

He was so taken aback at being right that he felt winded for a moment. He laughed breathily. "I don't know. Are you Irish Irish, or did your granny come from Ireland?"

She was still watching him measuringly. "I'm Irish Irish," she said. "And as it happens, my grandmother came from New York." Then she did stub out her cigarette, and pushed open the door of the bar behind her and, throwing him a cold, quick smile, was gone.

Now, in damp April, he was making his way into another bar, again in the Village, with something of the same sense of alarmed anticipation — though for different reasons — that he had felt when he had followed her into the dive on Houston Street that snowy afternoon in Christmas week, determined she would not disappear out of his life. She was standing at the bar, leaning on an elbow, holding a tall glass of something crimson. "What's up?" she said. "You're green round the gills." She was a painter, and she wore a painter's smock, but although she had been working and had come straight round from her studio on Bleecker Street there was not a spot of spilled paint to be seen anywhere on her person; she was not that kind of painter. She also wore leggings with black and grey horizontal stripes that made him think, incongruously, of Siena cathedral.

He ordered a dry martini, and Alison arched an eyebrow. "A bit early, isn't it?" she said. "What's the matter? Has your father-in-law cut you out of his will?"

Glass's connection with the Mulhollands was for Alison an unfailing invitation for raillery and comic elaboration. She was a humorous girl, with a wayward appreciation of life's more ridiculous arrangements. What she thought of his marriage to Louise he did not know, for she never said, which was fine by him. She painted big, bold abstracts in bright acrylics, which he did not consider very good. Alison knew what he thought of her work, and did not mind; she was that kind of painter.

He asked her what she was drinking, looking dubiously at the gory stuff in her glass, and she said it was a Virgin Mary. He sipped at his martini. She was waiting for him to tell her what it was that had made him speak to her so urgently, and so cryptically, on the telephone. Patience was one of her more notable qualities, patience, and a peculiar, and sometimes, so he found, unsettling way of becoming suddenly, eerily still, as if she were waiting calmly for something to take place that she had already foreseen.

"I think," he said, "I've got myself into a spot of bother."

She laughed. "Again?"

He took another go of his drink. He was trying to recall the exact moment when it had occurred to him that it would be a good idea to hire a researcher to help him in writing the Life of William Pius Mulholland. It had seemed such a simple, such an innocent, thing to do. "Did anyone phone you?" he asked.

"Did anyone *phone* me?" She pretended to ponder. "My mother rang the other day, to ask me how I am and if I've dumped you yet, which she is forever urging me to do. That dealer on Seventy-fourth Street called, but he's less interested in putting my pictures into his gallery than in getting into bed with me. And I spoke to the plumber about that leak in the —"

"I mean," Glass said, "anyone you didn't know. Anyone asking questions."

"What kind of questions?"

"Well, about us."

"*Us?*" She gave another, louder, laugh. "Who in this town knows about *us*?"

Her beauty assailed him afresh each time they met, yet it dismayed him, too. How would he bear it if he were to lose her? And lose her he would, of course, sooner or later. He found it hard to believe that he had got her in the first place. He had followed her into the bar that snowy December day and after a search had found her drinking Christmas tequilas with a couple of her girlfriends — tough broads, and how they had glared at him! — and spun her a transparently fake line about wanting to interview her for a piece he was supposed to be writing on the new Irish in Manhattan. She had gazed up at him in the solemn-faced way of someone trying not to laugh, and taken his card and braced it between a finger and thumb as if she were considering flipping it across the bar. Instead she had kept it and, to his surprise, telephoned him next morning and arranged a meeting in Washington Square at noon. She was, as he had guessed, a Dubliner, like him. Her father was dead, her mother worried about her endlessly, her brother was a banker and a bastard, she had been in New York a year, she lived in a freezing apartment above the Bleecker Street studio that her rich father had left her in his will — oh, and she had recently broken up with her boyfriend, a Romanian plasterer without a green card whose main interest in her, she had discovered, was the fact that she possessed an American passport thanks to her Brooklyn-born dad.

All this she had told him as they walked round the bare little park in the frost-smoke of the winter day. When he made to tell her something about himself she had said: "Oh, I know who you are. I've been reading you for years." He suspected that he had blushed.

Now, four months later, their affair had drifted into the doldrums, he could not quite say why. He loved her, in his way, and believed that she loved him, in her way, yet somehow they could not get a strong enough grip on each other; there was something that kept eluding them. Perhaps *in their way* was a way that was not direct enough, and that was why they seemed to keep swerving round each other. Then there was the fact that she resented the secrecy Glass had imposed on their liaison — that was the word he had once used to describe what they had going between them, and she had never forgotten or forgiven it — for he dreaded what would happen if his wife or, worse, his father-in-law, should hear of the affair. Not that it was the first time he had been unfaithful to Louise; nor was Louise herself a model of fidelity. The Glasses had an unspoken arrangement, eminently civilised, and Glass wanted to keep it that way. There were certain rules to be observed, the first of which was the rule of absolute discretion. Louise did not wish to know of his affairs, and emphatically not one that involved what seemed to be, all doubts and reservations aside, love, the actually existing thing itself.

"Go on," Alison said now, getting ready to laugh again, "you may as well tell me what's up." His supposed haplessness in the face of the world's difficulties was one of the things she claimed to love him for. This puzzled him and, although he would never say so, annoyed him, too, a little, for he had always thought of himself as quite a competent fellow, indeed, more than competent. Now, when he had finished telling her about Dylan Riley — telling her some of it, anyway — she did laugh, shaking her head. "Why do you call him the Lemur?" she asked. "And by the way, a lemur is not a rodent."

"How do you know?"

"I was a keen zoologist when I was at school. The name comes from the Latin word *lemures*, meaning ghosts, spectres."

"Anyway, he's that type, tall, gangly, with a long neck and shiny black eyes like my dear stepson's."

"You forget," Alison said drily, "that I've not had the opportunity to know what your dear stepson's eyes, or any other parts of him, look like."

Glass did not respond to this; in what circumstances could she possibly imagine him introducing her to David Sinclair? Standing next to them at the bar were a couple of caricature Wall Street brokers, loudly discussing hedge funds. One of them wore red braces — did brokers really wear red braces any more? — and had a big, square head like a side of beef.

"Anyway," Glass said, "I think the Lemur has found out about us. You're sure he didn't call?"

"Do you really think I would have forgotten if he had?"

He looked into his drink. "You mightn't want to tell me about it. I mean" — hastily — "you might have wanted to spare me."

"Spare you?" She laughed incredulously. "Well, he didn't. And I wouldn't. Want to spare you, that is." She drank the last of her drink. The beef-faced broker was eyeing her speculatively. "And now," she said, "I'm going back to work."

He took a taxi uptown, gazing out unseeingly at the damp blocks as they fleeted past. He was hungry, for in the bar he had taken nothing but two martinis, the famous New York liquid lunch. He thought of stopping off at the Bleeding Horse but decided he could not face the crowds and the venal leer of the maître d'.

Although he would never have admitted it, Glass was afraid of his father-in-law. His fear was of the low-key, fuzzy, four-o'clock-in-the-morning variety, always there, like the dread of death, a pilot light glowing steadily inside him. Big Bill had notoriously strong opinions on the sanctity of the marriage vow. He had managed to have his own first, brief, starry union annulled by the Vatican on technical grounds, while his second wife, the hard-riding Miz Claire, had come a conveniently fatal cropper; and although Nancy Harrison had left him twenty years ago, he still considered himself married to her. What would Big Bill do if he heard of his son-in-law's latest peccadillo? There had been scrapes in the past that Glass had managed to smooth over, with his wife's tight-lipped acquiescence, but Alison O'Keeffe, he was somehow certain, would be a different matter. What was to be done?

When he got out of the lift on the thirty-ninth floor he could hear the telephone ringing in his office. He fumbled the key into the door and scrambled to the desk and seized the receiver — What is it, he wondered, that is so irresistibly imperative about a ringing telephone?

"For God's sake," Louise said, "where have you been?" He mumbled something about lunch, and immediately, like retribution, an acid after-waft of gin burned his throat. "Someone has been phoning for you — he called twice, at least."

"Who?"

"A Captain Ambrose." Glass frowned in bafflement towards the transparent office wall and the deep canyons beyond. Why would someone in the army be calling him? Then he realised: it must be a policeman. Dear Christ.

"What did he want?"

"It seems someone has been killed."

Far uptown a speck-sized helicopter was hovering like a mosquito above a building site on the roof of a skyscraper, with a cable or something dangling from it, taut and straight, like a proboscis.

"Killed?" he said faintly.

"Yes. Murdered. What on earth have you been up to?"

CHAPTER
FIVE

Sweet Guys

The police station, if that was what to call it — headquarters? precinct house? — looked just as it would have in the movies. John Glass was led through a big, low-ceilinged, noisy room lined with desks and cramped cubicles, where many shirt-sleeved people, some in uniform and some not, walked determinedly about, carrying documents and paper coffee cups and shouting at each other. Glass idly entertained the fancy that, if it were viewed from above, all this apparently random toing and froing would resolve into a series of patterns, forming and re-forming, as in a Busby Berkeley musical. Everyone seemed to be either bored or in a temper. The women, washed-out blondes, mostly, were heavy-eyed and slow-moving, as if they had not slept last night, which perhaps they had not, since to Glass it appeared that every other working woman in New York City was a single mother, either divorced or abandoned. The big room had a somehow familiar aspect, which was more than just the memory of countless crime films, and after a minute or two it came to him: it looked exactly like a newspaper office.

Captain Ambrose had the face of an El Greco martyr, with deep-brown, suffering eyes and a nose like a finely honed stone axehead. He was tall and cadaverous, and his light-olive skin was smooth and seemingly hairless. Glass thought he might be an indian, Navajo, maybe, or Hopi. His accent was pure New York, though, broad-vowelled and nasal. He wore a dark-brown suit the same shade as his eyes, a white shirt and nondescript tie, and big black leather shoes with quarter-inch rims. There was nothing in the room that did not need to be there. The desk at which he sat showed him to be a fanatical tidier, with documents all sorted and squared, pens ranked by size and colour and every pencil freshly sharpened. On the wall were two framed photographs, of the President, and the late Pope John Paul II.

"Take a seat, Mr Glass," the policeman said. "Thanks for coming in."

A heavy-haunched woman with black roots showing in her butter-blonde hair entered without knocking and laid a sheaf of papers on the desk. "Think us two thirsty fellows could get a cup of coffee, Rhoda?" Captain Ambrose asked.

The woman glared at him. "Machine is bust," she said. "Walensky punched it again." She went out, and the glass panel in the door rattled behind her.

"How did you get my number?" Glass asked.

The policeman reached for the papers Rhoda had brought and held them upright and tapped them on the desk to align their edges. "It was in the call log on

Riley's cell phone," he said. "When did you speak to him?"

"This morning. At ten forty-seven." The captain lifted an eyebrow. "I happened to be looking at the clock."

"Ah. Right. That every witness should be so accurate."

Witness. The word sent something like a small electric charge along Glass's spine. It seemed to him that everything in the headachy, noise-assaulted, vertiginous six months he had lived in New York had been leading to just this moment, when he would be sitting here in this policeman's office, dry-mouthed and faintly nauseous, with a tingle in his backbone and his veins fizzing. What was happening was at once ordinary and outlandish, inevitable and contingent, as in a dream. "What happened?" he asked. "I mean, how did you . . .?"

The captain was leaning forward at the desk with his long narrow dark hands clasped before him, which intensified the sainted look. "His girlfriend called us. She'd been out of town, came back and found the body, still warm." Glass had not reckoned on Dylan Riley having a girlfriend. What kind of girl could she possibly be? The captain went on: "We're not getting much out of her at the moment, naturally. She didn't do it. We checked: she was in a Boeing somewhere over Pennsylvania when it happened. She says stuff was taken, two, maybe three computers."

"Then there must have been more than one person."

"Oh?"

"To be able to carry so much."

A faintly pitying light came into the policeman's eye. "Computers are compact and light these days, Mr Glass. That's why they're called laptops." He uncoiled himself from his chair, pushing down on the desk with the steepled fingers of one hand. He really was a very tall man. "Listen, I've got to get that cup of coffee. You want to come? There's a place across the street."

They moved in chill sunlight through the late-afternoon crowds. The captain loped along at a forward stoop, his arms slightly bowed and his head turned a little to the side, like an Indian scout, one of his ancestors, perhaps, leaning down intently to listen for the sound of the cavalry's distant hoof-beats. They were in the coffee shop before Glass thought of lighting up. A cigarette would have calmed him, but not much.

The place was crowded and while they were waiting for a table the policeman, jingling coins in a pocket of his trousers, talked in relaxed tones about the circumstances of Dylan Riley's death. Other customers, also waiting, stood within earshot, but paid no heed; apparently murder was a conversational commonplace, in the environs of Police Headquarters. "A very smooth job," the captain said. "Small-calibre bullet through the left eye. A Beretta, we think, maybe. Then the place was neatened up, with the victim on his bed and all, ready for the meat wagon. He was shot at his desk, though."

"How do you know that?"

Again the captain flashed that mild, pitying look. "Stains on the chair," he said. "Like the medical textbooks tell us: *no death without defecation.*"

A gum-chewing waitress in a gingham apron showed them to a table in a corner, the table-top was sticky to the touch. Glass really, really wanted a cigarette.

"You're Irish, right?" the captain said. "How long you been here?"

"Since November."

The ginghamed waitress brought their coffee.

"You planning on staying?"

"It seems so. My wife is American." The policeman nodded, and Glass saw that he knew a great deal more about him than the fact of his American wife. "My father-in-law has commissioned me to write his biography." It sounded entirely implausible. "That's William Mulholland."

Captain Ambrose nodded again, watching his hand as it spooned sugar into his cup. Glass felt he was back in a dream, trying to exonerate himself for some nameless thing he had not done, desperately offering up scraps of evidence to an omniscient but preoccupied and wholly unimpressible interrogator.

"I went to the Jesuits," the policeman said. Glass stared, helplessly, imagining himself a goldfish in a clouded bowl. What new tack was this? "St Peter's, in Jersey City. You know Jersey City? No, I guess not. You educated by the priests?"

"Mine was a diocesan college, in Ireland. Also called St Peter's, as it happens. Since in disgrace."

"Paedophiles? Right. We had them too. No one cared, in those days. And we never talked, I mean us kids — who would have listened?" He shook his head sadly. "Tough times."

"And not so long ago, either."

"That's right." He stirred his coffee slowly, slowly. Glass was trying to think which character in *Alice in Wonderland* the captain reminded him of. Was there a sloth? Or maybe the Caterpillar? And then at last the question came: "Tell me, Mr Glass, what was the connection with Dylan Riley?"

Glass heard himself swallow. "The connection?"

"Yeah, his connection with you, yours with him." He was still frowning into his cup, as if an answer might at any moment present itself there, etched in the froth. "Why was he phoning you?"

"As I said, I'm writing a biography of Mr Mulholland."

"A biography. Right."

"And Dylan Riley, he's — he was — a researcher. I had hired him — was thinking of hiring him — to work with me, on the book."

"Right," the policeman said again. "I figured that must be it."

After that there was a lengthy pause.

In his lifetime John Glass had known many occasions of fear. Once on a plane flying into Lebanon under Israeli rocket fire he had very nearly shat himself. It had been a humbling moment, never to be forgotten, or forgiven. What he felt now was not fear, exactly. His mouth was still dry, but he had a sensation deep in his gut that was as much excitement as anxiety. He was, in a strange way, he realised, thrilled: thrilled to be mixed up in a murder, thrilled to be here being questioned by this peculiar lawman, thrilled that, somehow, after all these months, he could be said to have really arrived at last in New York, this place that was so vividly, so violently, so murderously alive. He recalled a phrase from Emerson about death, and us thinking of it: *there at least is reality that will not dodge us.*

He drank the bitter black coffee. "Where did he live," he asked, "Dylan Riley?"

"SoHo, near the river. He had a warehouse on Vandam, filled with all this surveillance stuff. Remember Gene Hackman in *The Conversation?* I suspect our boy was a keen movie-goer."

"They say he was very good at what he did."

"That right? Who's *they?*"

Glass retracted instantly, like a touched snail. "Some people I know — journalists. That's how I got his name."

The captain had taken out a gunmetal cigarette lighter and was turning it idly in his fingers. A fellow smoker! Glass experienced a rush of brotherly warmth for this long, emaciated, saintly-seeming figure. Ambrose saw him looking hungrily at the lighter and grinned. "Gave them up six months ago — about the time you moved here to our fair and wondrous city." He shifted sideways on his chair to allow his long legs more space. The espresso machine behind the bar began to hiss like an industrial boiler and he had to raise his voice to be heard. "My problem is, Mr Glass, somebody shot this Dylan Riley, which means somebody had a reason to shoot him, and I don't know what that reason might be. He was a researcher, you say, but from the look of the inside of that warehouse of his he was a lot more than that, or aspired to be." He picked up his empty cup and peered into it regretfully, as if there would never be another drink of coffee to be had. His eyes were hooded. "Secrets, Mr Glass," he said. "Dangerous things."

Another silence followed. The policeman kept his eyes downcast and seemed to be pondering the woes of the world.

"I don't think," Glass said, measuring his words, "that I can help you, Captain. I didn't know Dylan Riley, not in any real sense."

Those olive-dark lids shot up and the eyes fixed him, wet-brown and shining. "But you met him." It was not a question.

"Yes, I — he — that is, he came to my office, to discuss the possibility of his working with me on the book. Nothing was agreed."

The policeman was still watching him. "What kind of research would you have wanted him to do, if something had been 'agreed'?"

Glass's nerves were thrumming for the want of a cigarette. "Just . . . general. Dates, places, people Mr Mulholland met, where, when. That kind of thing."

The captain flipped open the lid of the lighter but did not ignite the flame. Glass caught a faint whiff of gas from the pinprick nozzle, or imagined that he did, and his craving nerves stretched another notch.

"Mr Mulholland," the captain said, "is a pretty interesting man. That's to say, he's led a pretty interesting life. Must be some things in his past you won't be able to write about."

"There are things in all our pasts that wouldn't bear the light of day."

The policeman gave a low, deprecating laugh. "But that's not the same thing, is it? What I mean is, Mr Mulholland is likely to have secrets that wouldn't be *allowed* to see the light of day. Given his line of work before he set up Mulholland Cable."

"Then I'm wasting my time."

That seemed to require no comment, and again a silence fell between the two men, uneasy, and faintly rancorous. Glass was calculating the number of lies he had told the policeman so far today. Or not lies, perhaps, in the strict sense, the sense the Jesuits of St Peter's in Jersey City would have insisted on, but shifted emphases, strategic withholdings. What was the phrase? Sins of omission? That was it. Yet it was no task of his to incriminate himself. He paused on that thought. Incriminate himself in what? He had not shot Dylan Riley. All he was doing was trying to cover up the possibility, the distinct possibility, that what the Lemur had unearthed was the fact of Glass's affair with Alison O'Keeffe, and that he had been out to blackmail Glass by threatening to reveal the affair to his wife and her father. What man, what husband, no matter how far estranged from his wife, would not want to suppress such a revelation and preserve the arrangement that had been suiting everyone for so long? And then, deny the thought though he might, there was that million dollars . . .

"I read that thing you wrote," the captain said, "that thing in one of the magazines, about the Menendez brothers." Glass stared, and the captain rolled his

49

scarecrow's shoulders in a parody of prideful shyness. "Shucks, yeah, I read, don't even move my lips." He stirred his coffee again. "It was a good piece. Lyle and Erik. Sweet guys. You meet them?"

"I did."

"And?"

"Sweet guys."

The captain chuckled, and pushed aside his cup and stood up. Together they went towards the door. Glass brought out his wallet but the policeman lifted a hand. "We don't pay here," he said, with stony emphasis. "Graft. Don't you know about New York cops?" Then he grinned. "Joke. I keep a tab open."

In the street Glass paused to light a cigarette, and the captain stood with his hands in his pockets and watched him, shaking his head. "You should quit," he said. "Believe me, it makes a difference. Even in the sack — you got more breath."

They waited at the lights and then crossed.

"Mr Mulholland know about you and Dylan Riley?" the policeman asked.

"There wasn't much to know."

They were at the door of the station. Glass was unsure if he was free to go; maybe the real questioning had not started yet. He had so far only met the good cop, surely the bad one would be along any minute. The captain stopped, and turned to him. "You know you were the last person Dylan Riley called? That makes you the last one to talk to him alive."

"You mean, the second last."

Captain Ambrose grinned again. "Yeah. Right."

CHAPTER
SIX

All Hands!

John Glass disliked the sprawling apartment where he and his wife lived, more or less. More or less, in that Louise lived there, while he merely joined her in the evenings, stayed overnight, and left in the mornings. That, at least, was how he thought of it. To an observer — and the wealthy and fashionable Mrs Glass was always under scrutiny — the Glasses would have seemed a typical Upper East Side couple. Louise made sure that it should stay that way. She was careful to preserve appearances not least for fear of her father and what he would do if she allowed a scandal to develop. William Mulholland's bitter disapproval of divorce was well known, and he had been heard to accuse his daughter, no more than half jokingly, of being a bigamist. Big Bill had not much liked Rubin Sinclair, Louise's first husband, but, as she later told Glass one champagne-lit night when they were first together, he had liked it even less when she announced, no doubt with a quaver of terror in her voice, that the marriage had gone hopelessly awry and that she was filing for divorce. Her father had not argued with her, Louise said in some wonderment, had not shouted or threatened. The mildness of his response had been more frightening to her than any show of rage. "You took a vow, Lou," he had said gravely. "You took a vow, and now you're breaking it."

After the divorce came through Louise had fled with her ten-year-old son to Ireland, to her father's big old Georgian house in Connemara, to tend her soul's wounds and figure out how to rebuild her life. In Ireland she had met John Glass — for the first time, as she had thought, for she had forgotten that long-ago wind-blown afternoon at the nearby Huston place — and something about him, a detached, dreamy something, had seemed the perfect balm for her bruised spirit. John Glass was everything that Rubin Sinclair was not. Or so she had thought. For his part, John Glass was certain, despite all he knew of Fate and her caprices, that the fact of this exquisite creature's having drifted a second time into his orbit was a circumstance to be seized upon without delay. He had proposed three months previously, on the same date that her divorce had come through. "Oh, God," Louise said, a laughing wail, "what will my father say!"

Once again Big Bill's response had been unexpectedly mild. He liked, it seemed, John Glass. He still had friends in the surveillance world and had got them to look into his past — "Don't mind it, son, it's an old habit" — and was satisfied with what was turned up. Glass had never been married, and therefore not divorced, he was admired in his profession, seemed honest, and was probably not a fortune-hunter. "Just one thing," Big Bill had said to his daughter and her prospective husband, with a smile that seemed only mildly pained, "wait to marry until you're at least a year divorced, Lou, to save what shreds of respectability our poor old family has left." And Louise had kissed him. Kissing was not a thing they often did, Big Bill and his daughter.

John Glass was remembering that kiss when he entered the lobby of the apartment building after his interview with Captain Ambrose. He could not recall what thoughts had gone through his head as he watched that unwonted moment of intimacy and accord between father and daughter, and this troubled him. But perhaps he had not been thinking anything. His memories of those days were all hazed over happily, as if he were looking back through a pane of glass that had been breathed on by someone who was laughing.

Lincoln, the doorman, tipped his cap and remarked on the weather. "Be getting warmer soon, Mr Glass, and then we be wishing for the cool days again." There was a touch of the poet to old Lincoln.

Glass went up in the little elevator. It was a venerable and somewhat rackety contraption, and he was never comfortable in it, feeling constricted and vaguely at peril. He refused to let himself make of this a metaphor for his life in general. He was a free man, no matter how narrow his circumstances might have become recently. Yes, free.

The elevator opened directly on to a private hallway leading into the apartment. The first time he had entered here he had been more impressed, cowed, even, than he would have cared to admit. Now he called out, "All hands!" as he always did; he could not remember the origin of this manner of announcing his homecoming. From far inside the apartment he heard Louise's muted answering call. He found her in the library, seated at her desk, an eighteenth-century escritoire, with a little pile of cards and envelopes, and her fountain pen. She was wearing the grey silk kimono that some Japanese bigwig had presented to her when she visited Kyoto as a UN Special Ambassador for Culture. She gave her husband a glancing, absent-minded smile. "There you are," she said, and went back to her cards.

He stood behind her. He caught her sharp perfume. What was the word? Civet. The same perfume smells differently on every woman. Or so he had been told. He felt curiously unfocused, adrift, somehow. He supposed it was the aftermath of his meeting with Captain Ambrose, and all the adrenalin he had used up. "What are you doing?" he asked.

"Invitations for Tuesday."

"Tuesday?"

"The party for Antonini."

"Oh. The painter."

"Yes," she said, imitating his flat tone. "The painter."

"I think he has a soft spot for you."

She did not turn, or lift her head. "Do you?"

"Or a hard spot, more likely."

"Don't be coarse."

"That's me, coarse as cabbage."

54

He admired the way she wrote, in firm, swift strokes, so confidently. He had not used a fountain pen since he was in primary school.

Why did she not ask about the call from Captain Ambrose? Could she have forgotten?

He moved away and sat down on the low white sofa, where he was surrounded on three sides by bookshelves reaching to the ceiling. It struck him that he had not lifted a volume from those shelves since . . . since he could not remember when. They stood there, the books, sorted, ranked, a battalion of rebukes. He had not done that book of his own that he had always planned to do. The unwritten book: another cliché.

"By the way," Louise said, and still did not turn, "did you speak to that policeman?"

"Yes."

"What was it about? *Was* someone murdered?"

"Yes."

Now she did turn, setting an elbow on the back of her chair and looking at him with a faint, questioning smile. "Someone we know?" she said lightly.

He put his head back on the cushions and considered first one corner of the ceiling, then another. "No."

When he failed to continue she waggled her head in a parody of regal impatience and said, "Weh-ell?" in her Queen Victoria voice. He lowered his gaze and fixed it on her. Her eyes shone, and her glossed lips caught points of light from the chandelier above his head and glittered. Why was she excited? It must be, he thought, the prospect of the smouldering Antonini. He went back to gazing at the ceiling.

"A young man called Dylan Riley," he said. "Computer wizard. Would-be spy." *And? Go on, say it.* "Researcher."

"And the police were calling you why?"

"He had phoned me, this Riley."

"He had phoned you."

"Yes. This morning. And in the afternoon he was killed. Murdered. Shot through the eye."

"My God." She sounded more indignant than shocked. "But why was he phoning you, this person — what did you say his name was?"

"Riley. Dylan Riley. Doesn't sound like a real name, does it, when you say it out loud?"

He picked up a copy of the *New Yorker* from the low table in front of him. Sempé. The Park, spring leaves, a tiny dog.

"Are you," Louise said, "going to tell me what this is about, or not?"

"It's not *about* anything. I contacted this Riley because I thought he might do some research for the book. He called me back. Mine happened to be the last number on his mobile phone. Hence the call from the police." She still sat turned towards him from the waist, her arm still resting on the back of the chair, the fountain pen in her fingers. "The nib will dry up," he said. "I remember that, how the nib would dry up and then you had to wash it out with water and fill it in the inkwell again."

"The *inkwell*?" she said. "You sound like someone out of Dickens."

"I *am* someone out of Dickens. That's why you married me. Bill Sikes, *c'est moi.*"

Clara the maid came in to announce dinner. She was a diminutive person. Her colour, deep black with purplish shadings, fascinated Glass; every time he saw her he wanted to touch her, just to know the feel of that satiny skin. In her little white uniform and white rubber-soled shoes that Louise made her wear she had the look of a hospital nurse. When she was gone, Louise whispered: "You must remember to compliment her. She's made a soufflé. It's a big moment." Louise had been teaching Clara how to cook, with considerable success, which was fortunate for Clara, since otherwise she would have gone by now — Louise did not entertain failure.

In the dining room the lamps burned low, and there were candles on the table, their flames reflected in countless gleaming spots among the silver and the crystal. It occurred to Glass that what he had admitted a moment ago was true, that he *was* coarse, compared to all this that Louise had set in place, the elegant table, the soft lights, the fine wines and delicate food, the expensively simple furniture, the Balthus drawing and the Giacometti figurine, the leather-bound books, the white-clad maid, the Glenn Gould tape softly playing in the background — all the rich, muted, exquisitely tasteful life that she had assembled for them. Yes, he fitted ill, here; he had tried, but he fitted ill. He wondered why she had tolerated him for so long, and why she went on tolerating him. Was it simply fear of another divorce and her father's rage? No doubt it was. He was perfectly capable, was Big Bill, of cutting off her inheritance. So much would go, for her and for David Sinclair, if those millions went — not just the house in the Hamptons, the rooftop suite at the George V in Paris, the account at Asprey's in London but, most importantly, control of the Mulholland Trust. That was what Louise prized most; that was the future.

Clara's spinach soufflé was excellent, and Glass remembered to compliment her on it, and she fled back to her kitchen in confusion. Louise had put down her fork and was gazing at him. "You can be so sweet sometimes," she said.

"Only sometimes?"

"Yes. Only sometimes. But I'm grateful."

"Don't mention it."

Still she watched him, at once frowning and smiling. "You *have* been up to something," she said, "haven't you? I can see it in your eye."

"What sort of something?"

Her face, candlelit, was reflected in the window by which she sat. Outside in the darkness the crowns of the massed trees in the Park gave off an eerie, silverish glow. "I don't know," she said. "Something to do with that young man who was murdered?"

"What?" Glass said. "Do you think I shot him?"

"Of course not. Why would you?"

A sudden, constrained silence fell then, as if both had taken fright at something vaguely seen ahead. They ate.

Glass poured the wine. At length he said: "I don't know that I can write this book."

She kept her eyes on her plate. "Oh? Why not?"

"Well, for a start I suddenly remembered that I am a journalist, or used to be, and not a biographer."

"Journalists write biographies."

"Not of their fathers-in-law, they don't."

"Billuns gave his word he wouldn't interfere."

"Billuns" was Big Bill's pet-name in the family; it made Glass's skin crawl, especially when his wife used it. He drank his wine and looked out over the treetops. How still it was, the April night.

"Why do you think he asked me to write it? I mean, why *me*?"

"He told you himself: he trusts you."

"Does that mean more, I wonder, than that he thinks he has a hold over me, through you?"

"*Thinks*?" She smiled, pursing her lips. "Doesn't he have a hold over you, through me?"

He looked at her levelly in the candlelight. He did not understand why she was behaving so tenderly towards him tonight. There was a languorous, almost feline air about her. He was reminded of how, on their honeymoon, which seemed so long ago now, she would sit opposite him at a balcony table in the Eden Roc at Cap d'Antibes after a morning of lovemaking and smile at him in that same caressing, mischievous fashion, and kick off her sandals under the table and wrap her cool bare feet round his ankles. What days those had been, what nights. At moments such as this one now, here in the stealthy candlelight, the sadness he felt at the lapsing of his love for her became a desolation. He cleared his throat. "Tell me," he said, "about Charles Varriker."

Something flickered in her eyes, a far-off lightning flash. "Charles?" she said. "Why?"

"I don't know. He's a figure in the landscape — your father's landscape."

Her mood had altered now: she seemed impatient, angry, almost. "He's been dead for twenty years, more."

"How well did you know him? Was he a figure in *your* landscape?"

She put down her fork again and lowered her head and turned it a little to one side; it was a thing she did when she was thinking, or upset. "Is this how it's going to be if you write this book?" she asked, in an odd, low voice with a shake in it. "Will there be dinner-table interrogations? Will I be required nightly to pick over the past for you? A pity your researcher got shot, he would have spared me a lot of work." She rose abruptly, not looking at him. Her napkin had fallen to the floor and she found herself treading on it. "Damn!" she said, in that same, angry undertone, and kicked the napkin off into the shadows, and strode away, the skirts of the kimono ruffling about her. Glass thought to call after her but did not. The silence seemed to vibrate faintly, as in the aftermath of something having shattered.

What had Dylan Riley discovered, and why had he been shot? And how were the two things connected, as Glass was now convinced they were? He looked again to the window, but this time saw only his own face reflected there.

CHAPTER
SEVEN

The Cleaver

John Glass woke early out of a riot of vivid and disorderly dreams, all detailed recollection of which drained from his mind the moment he opened his eyes. He lay in the half-dark feeling paralysed by dread. What was the matter, what terrible thing was amiss? Then he remembered the murder of Dylan Riley, the black weight of which lay over him like a shroud. How was it he could have been so calm yesterday, so detached, when he heard of the young man's killing and Captain Ambrose summoned him to Police Headquarters? He marvelled, not for the first time, at how the self insulates and protects itself against life's shocks. He closed his eyes again, tight, and burrowed down into the warmth of the bedclothes and his own familiar fetor. He knew that things would seem different when the sun came up and the ordinary business of the day began. For now, though, he could have done with someone else's warmth beside him, another's body to cling to for solace. But Louise had long ago, and without fuss, banished him from the master bedroom into the box-room at the end of the corridor beyond the library. The arrangement suited him; mostly he preferred to sleep alone, if sleep was all that was going to happen, and it was some time since anything else had happened in bed between him and Louise.

He tried to fall back to sleep but could not. His mind was racing. It felt as if he were not so much thinking as being thought. Memories, nameless forebodings, speculations and conjectures, all were jumbled together in the ashen afterglow of the dreams he had forgotten. He turned on his back and lay gazing up at the shadowed ceiling. As so often late at night or in the early-morning hours he asked himself if he had made a mistake in moving from Ireland to America — no, not if he had made a mistake, but how great were the proportions of the mistake he had made. Not that he and Louise had been so very much happier living in Ireland, in Louise's father's gloomy grey-stone mansion at Mount Ardagh, and not that they had seen so very much of each other, for that matter. They had both spent the greater part of their time travelling, he on assignments abroad and Louise promoting charities across five continents. He knew he should not but in his heart he despised his wife's career, so-called, as an ambassador of good works.

Maybe they should have had children.

He shifted, groaning angrily. The pillow was too hot, and his pyjama top was damp with sweat and held him fast like a strait-jacket. He could hear Clara in the kitchen, getting her mistress's day started — Louise was an early riser. It made him uneasy, having a live-in servant. His father had died young and his widowed mother had kept house for a rich Dublin lawyer so that her only son could have an education. *Coarse*, he thought again, *coarse as cabbage*. He sighed. It was time to get up.

Dylan Riley's murder was not reported in the *Times*, or at any rate he could find no mention of it. Louise would not have the *Post* or the *Daily News* in the house so he had to go out and buy them. He took them into his workroom — where he never did any work — and sat on the silk-covered *chaise-longue* that Louise had bought for him as a house-warming gift when they had moved in here six months ago. The *Post* had a couple of paragraphs on the killing, but the *News* ran a bigger story, on page five: *Computer Whiz's Mystery Slaying*. There was nothing in either report that was new. Captain Ambrose of the NYPD was quoted as saying that he and his team were following a number of definite leads. There was a photograph of Riley's girlfriend, one Terri Taylor, leaving the premises on Vandam in the company of a policewoman. She wore jeans and had long black hair; she had turned her face away from the cameras.

He switched on the miniature television set that squatted on a corner of his desk. There was an item on Fox 5 news, just a plain reporting of the facts. New York 1 had sent a camera and a reporter, and there was footage of Terri Taylor briefly on the pavement outside the warehouse. She was a pale, waif-like creature with a little pointed face and haunted eyes. She did not seem entirely heartbroken; rather, her look was one of bafflement and dismay, as if she were wondering dazedly how she had come to be involved in this mess.

The camera team had managed to corner Captain Ambrose. On screen he looked even more like a tormented saint, in his brown suit and his big black brogues. He talked here also of "definite leads", and then walked away quickly from the camera at his indian-scout lope. Common to all the reports of the murder was an underlying note of — not indifference, exactly, but of half-heartedness, and faint impatience, as if everybody felt that time was being wasted here, while matters of far greater import were calling out urgently for attention elsewhere. What this meant, Glass knew, was that no one expected the murder to be solved. Dylan Riley had been a loner, according to the *Daily News*, so there would be no one to press the police for action. Even Terri Taylor, it was obvious, was leaving the scene as fast as her skinny legs would take her.

Glass went into the kitchen to get himself a cup of coffee and a piece of toast, but Clara was there and of course insisted on doing it for him. He stood leaning against the refrigerator pretending to read the sports pages of the *Daily News*. Louise had already breakfasted and left — she had a meeting at the United Nations with someone from UNESCO. Glass wondered idly if his wife ever met anyone who was not someone. Covertly he watched Clara as she bustled about the windowless room. He knew almost nothing about her life. Her people were from the Caribbean — Puerto Rico, was it, or the Dominican Republic? He could not remember. She had a boyfriend, according to Louise, but so far there had been so sightings of the ghostly lover. What did she do in the evenings, he wondered, in her room off the kitchen? Watched television, he supposed. Did she read, and if so, what? He could not imagine. It struck him that for a journalist he felt very little curiosity about people, how they thought, what they felt. Dylan Riley, for instance; what did he know of him, except that he resembled a lemur and did not wash often enough? Maybe that was why he had given up journalism, he thought, because fundamentally he had scant concern for human beings. It was events that interested him, things happening, not those involved.

Clara handed him his coffee. "Real strong, Mr Glass, like you like it." She smiled, flashing her shiny white teeth. The toast had the texture of scorched plaster of Paris.

The day outside was fresh and blustery, and there was a lemony cast to the sunlight. He took a taxi to Forty-fourth Street to check his mail. As usual, there was none. He sat with his feet on his desk and his hands behind his head and studied the sky, or what he could spy of it, between the jumbled buildings. He believed he could see the wind, faint striations like scour-marks etched on the clear blue. He wished he could feel something solid and real about Dylan Riley's murder — anger, indignation, an itch of curiosity, even. Yet all he could think was that Riley was dead and what did it matter who had killed him?

Then he remembered something, and he shifted his feet from the desk and reached for the telephone, fishing Captain Ambrose's card out of his wallet.

When he said his name the policeman betrayed no surprise. Was he looking out at the same sky, that streaked azure?

"Who else did Dylan Riley call?" Glass asked. "Before he called me, I mean."

There was a breathy sound on the line that might have been a low laugh. "Called lots of people," the policeman said. "You thinking of anyone in particular?"

"I mean, did you trace all the numbers on his phone? Did you identify them all?"

"Sure, we traced them. His girlfriend, his dental hygienist, his mother in Orange County down in Florida. And you."

"No one else in my family? Not my father-in-law?"

"Mr Mulholland? No. You think he might have called him about this research you wanted him to do?"

"I expressly told him not to."

"You said Mr Mulholland didn't know you were bringing in someone to check out his history."

Glass closed his eyelids briefly and pressed an index finger to his forehead. "I told you, I hadn't decided finally whether to hire Riley or not."

"Right. So you did, I remember." There was a silence; it hummed in Glass's ear. The policeman said: "You were the one he called — twice. That's why I asked you to come in. You were the only one we couldn't account for, the only one who wasn't his girlfriend or his dentist or his mother." Another pause. "You got something you want to tell me, Mr Glass? About Mr Mulholland, maybe?"

"No," Glass said, and expelled a breath. "I was just curious."

"And worried?"

"Worried?"

"That Riley might have let your father-in-law know you had hired — were thinking of hiring — a snoop."

"No," Glass said, making his voice go dull. "I wasn't worried." He could sense the captain thinking, turning over the possibilities. "Mr Mulholland and I have an understanding. He trusts me."

Again there was that snuffle of suppressed amusement. "But you hadn't told him about Dylan Riley."

"I would have," Glass said, still in that dulled, dogged tone.

"Sure, Mr Glass. Sure you would."

When he had put down the receiver he sat for a long time drumming his fingers on the desk and gazing unseeing before him, trying to think. His mind was still fogged with the after-traces of last night's unremembered dreams. He picked up the phone again and called Alison O'Keeffe and asked if she would have an early lunch with him. She said she was in the middle of work but he pressed her and in the end she gave in, as he had known she would. He telephoned for a table at Pisces, a little fish place down at Union Square that had been a favourite haunt of theirs in the early days of their affair. Like Mario's, it was becoming depressingly fashionable, and Glass worried that some day Louise would come in with one of her someones in tow and find him and

Alison all snug and cosy at their accustomed corner table. *That* would be awkward.

He had not spoken to Alison since yesterday. He did not like to think of her being involved, however peripherally, in the business of Dylan Riley's death, and was sorry he had mentioned Riley to her in the first place. He still could not think how Riley might have found out about him and Alison; he supposed he was naïve for having imagined that New York was big and impersonal enough to allow him to carry on a love affair without anyone knowing.

In the restaurant he sat at the table with his back to the wall and watched the door, impatient with himself for his nervousness. So what if Louise should appear and find him with Alison? They were not children, they knew about each other's lives. Probably if she did come in she would merely sweep the room rapidly in that way she did and let her glance glide over the happy couple and then change her table to one as far from theirs as possible.

In his honour Alison had exchanged her painter's smock for a skirt and a blue silk blouse. When she kissed him he caught behind her perfume a faint whiff of acrylics; the smell always reminded him of brand-new toys at Christmas time. He waited for her to mention Dylan Riley but she did not; she must not have seen the news of his death. She wore her hair drawn tightly back from her face and tied at the nape of her neck with an elastic band. She touched his hand, smiling, and asked what it was they were celebrating. "Nothing," he said. "Us." She nodded, sceptically, still smiling with lowered eyelashes; she knew about Glass and spontaneity.

They ate Chilean sea bass and green salad, and Glass ordered a bottle of Tocai from Friuli, even though Alison had said she wanted to work in the afternoon and would drink only water. He downed the first glass of wine in two long draughts and poured another before the bossy waiter had time to wrest the bottle out of his hand. Alison, watching him, frowned. "Why are you so edgy?" she asked. "You'll be drunk in a minute, and I'll have to carry you home to your wife."

She was right: the wine had gone straight to his head already. As he looked at her, seated there before him with the crowded room at her back, she appeared to shine, in her blue blouse, a living, blood-warm creature. It seemed to him he had never noticed her ears before, these intricate, whorled, funny and lovable things attached at either side of her dear face. He wanted to reach across the table and touch her. He wanted to hold her head, that frail and delicate egg, between his palms and kiss her and tell her he loved her. Tears were welling in his eyes and the back of his throat was swollen. He felt ridiculous and happy. He was alive, and here, with his girl, in the midst of the cheerful clamour of midday, and it was spring, and he would live forever.

"By the way," she said, "do you know someone called Cleaver?"

He blinked. "What? No. Who?"

She gave him a frowning smile that made her nose wrinkle at the bridge. "Cleaver," she said. "Wilson Cleaver." She shook her head. "What a name."

He was having some difficulty with his breathing. "Who is he?"

"I don't know."

"What do you mean, you don't know?"

"He's a journalist, I think. A reporter. He telephoned me yesterday, just after you did. He wanted to talk to you. I thought it was odd."

He stared at her. The tipsy euphoria of a minute ago had evaporated entirely. "How did he get your number?"

"I think he knows that fellow you were talking about yesterday. What's his name? Someone Dylan? No — Dylan someone."

"Riley."

"That's it. Dylan Riley. What was it you called him?"

"The Lemur."

CHAPTER
EIGHT

The Sheepfold

They had arranged to meet by the Boathouse in the
Park. On the telephone Glass had listened intently to
Wilson Cleaver's voice but had not learned a great deal
from it. Black, he thought, from the jivey bounce in the
tone and the way he dealt with certain sibilants.
Self-confident, too, with an overlay of easy, almost
languid, amusement. If he had been a friend of Dylan
Riley's he certainly did not seem to be in mourning.
"Good of you to call, Mr Glass," he had said, with a
lordly, laughing air. "I know your stuff, of course. Been
a fan of yours for years." There had been no mention of
Riley or his death. All very businesslike. The Boathouse,
noon. "See you there, Mr Glass. Look forward to it."

At twelve on the stroke he came striding along by the
water, smiling and with a hand thrust out while he was
still five yards off. "Mr Glass, I presume?" he said.
"Cleaver. Howdy do?" He was a young man, thin and
tall with a sharp face and a big, exaggerated smile. His
hair was cut close and he sported a sort of beard that
was just two narrow black lines running down past his
ears and along the jaw-line to meet underneath the
notched chin. He wore a striped seersucker jacket

71

tightly buttoned and a blue bow-tie with red polka dots. Glass noticed his shoes, impossibly long and narrow patent-leather sheaths, the laces knotted into stiff and perfectly formed figures-of-eight. There was something about him of the professional performer, but one from another age, a sixties stand-up comedian, maybe, or even one of those old-time zoot-suited jazzmen with a horn in one hand and a reefer in the other. He was all movement, flexing his knees and shooting his cuffs and tugging at his tie, as if he were controlled by an internal clockwork mechanism, oiled and intricate. Having shaken hands with Glass he smoothed the wings of his sleek, pencil moustache rapidly downwards with the tips of a thumb and forefinger. "Let's walk," he said.

The day had a bluey-green tinge and the coming of spring was everywhere in evidence. The trees quivered and there were fresh gusts of wind among the budding boughs, and the lake water shone like a knife-blade. Glass loved this park, so grand, so generous and so unexpected. Today, as always, there were joggers everywhere, and young mothers airing their children, or perhaps they were not mothers but minders, and the usual complement of crazy people and shuffling down-and-outs.

"How that book of yours coming along?" Cleaver asked.

"What book?"

Cleaver had a high-pitched, hiccupy laugh. "Oo, you so coy!" he crowed.

"How do you know me?" Glass asked coldly. "How did you come to have Alison O'Keeffe's number?"

"I thought it was *your* number, man. Old Dylan, he liked to think he was real organised but he sure could get his data mixed up."

"You knew him, then, Dylan Riley?"

"Yeah, I knew him, the poor cracker."

"What do you do, Mr Cleaver?"

"I do what you do, Mr Glass."

"You're a journalist?"

"Paid up and bona fidee."

Glass had understood from the start that the Dixie slang and the cornpone accent were put on. Cleaver was making fun of him.

"You know Riley is dead."

Cleaver made a gun of a thumb and forefinger and pointed it at his eye. "No great surprise, and he can't claim he wasn't warned. 'Riley,' I'd say to him, 'you not careful, you going to get yourself whacked someday, boy.' But would he listen? No, sir."

They came in sight of the Bethesda Fountain with its gilded angel striding aloft. Two little boys were wrestling by the parapet of the fountain, each trying to topple the other into the water, while a bored young woman with an Eastern European pallor looked on listlessly.

"See, what it is," Cleaver said, as if continuing a topic already opened, "I wrote some things about your Mr Mulholland for *Slash* —" He broke off. "You know that magazine, man, that *Slash*? No? It's good. Small, sure, but it's sharp, like you might guess from the name. Anyways, I got leaned on pretty hard for those things I wrote. Yeah, pretty hard."

A large dark bird flew down swiftly from the trees on their right and skimmed the footpath with wings outspread.

"What do you mean, leaned on?" Glass asked.

"Oh, you know. Silence all of a sudden from certain quarters that used to be real noisy. Commissions cancelled with no reason given. Phone calls at four in the morning with nobody saying anything only breathing real heavy. You get my drift?"

"And you think Mr Mulholland was behind these things?"

"It's a fair bet, don't you think?"

"No, I don't."

Cleaver found this funny and did his heehaw laugh. "Fact," he said, "I was planning to write a book about him. Ain't that a coincidence, you and me both on the same track? 'Cept my book would have been different from yours, I'm guessing."

"You were going to write a biography of Mr Mulholland?"

"Not exactly. More a exposé, you might say. I been real interested in him for a long time. And in Charles Varriker, his guy that died all those years ago. Dylan Riley, he was helping me. I hired him, like you did." So, Glass thought, that's how Riley happened to have all those facts at his fingertips about Big Bill. "Yeah, he was in on it with me for a while, until I gave it up, under all that pressure from persons unknown. And now he's dead. There's another coincidence."

They came to the Bow Bridge and set off across it, towards the Ramble.

"What's your interest in Charles Varriker?" Glass asked.

"Well, he's the main man in the story of Big Bill's financial recovery way back then in the bad old eighties, ain't he? He was the one Big Bill brought in to save Mulholland Cable when Mr Bankruptcy began to beckon. Now Varriker, what I know of him, wasn't the kind of man who'd let himself get so low there wasn't nothing for it but to eat a gun."

"You think his death wasn't suicide?"

"What *you* think?"

They had come to the middle of the bridge, and Cleaver stopped and turned his head to look both ways along the water. "Handsomest spot in all Manhattan," he said. "You know this bridge was built by the same company that made the dome of the Capitol in Washington, D.C.? That's the kind of thing I know, see. Useless information that one day suddenly becomes useful. Like knowing, for instance, that on the day before the day that Charles Varriker died — May seventeenth, 1984, which was a Thursday, case you're interested — he bought a first-class round-trip ticket to Paris, France. Kind of a odd thing to do for a man contemplating offing himself, don't you think, Mr Glass?"

They walked on. A wind was rising and the trees on the bank before them swayed and hissed, swayed and hissed. A bundle of cloud was swelling slowly over the pinnacles of Fifth Avenue.

"Why Bill Mulholland?" Glass asked.

"How's that?"

"Why were you so interested in him in the first place? Have you met him?"

"Never had that pleasure, no."

"Probably you'd find he's not what you think he is."

"Which would be?"

They turned south, walking under the unquiet trees. The sunlight was fading, and the air had taken on a chill.

"Do you suspect," Glass asked, "that Mr Mulholland had a hand in Dylan Riley's murder?"

Cleaver put on a shocked look and lifted his hands and wagged them from side to side. "Lordy, Mr Glass," he said, hamming it up shamelessly, "the things you do ask! And I thought I was bad-minded."

"But do you?"

Cleaver squinted at the clouding sky. "Well now, let's consider. I write some less than warm opinions of your Mr Mulholland, and in particular the much-acclaimed Mulholland Trust, and all sorts of shit starts happening to my professional life. Then you come along and ask my late, lamented colleague Dylan Riley to do a little snooping into your father-in-law's interesting and highly colourful life, and before you can say 'dirty linen' he gets a cap put in his eye. I'd call that suspicious, Mr Glass, yes, I surely would."

Glass felt cold suddenly, and buttoned up his jacket and shoved his hands into the pockets. Cleaver, beside him, was humming a tune lightly under his breath and clicking his tongue at intervals.

"Dylan Riley telephoned me," Glass said, "the day he was killed. He had found out something. He wouldn't say what it was. He tried to blackmail me."

Cleaver threw back his head and hooted. "That Riley!" he said delightedly. "He sure was some tease. What did he try to hit you for?"

"Half a million dollars."

"Whee! You can't fault him for lack of daring. Half a million bucks! Whatever it was he found out it must have been something. He give you no clue what it was?"

"No." Glass paused, and then said: "I thought you might know."

"Me?" Cleaver looked at him wide-eyed, seeming genuinely startled. "How would I know? Dylan and me, we weren't that close. He was kind of tight-fisted on the information front."

There was a light spatter of rain and they turned back towards the bridge.

"Whatever it was he stumbled on may not have been about Bill Mulholland," Glass said carefully.

"No?"

"No. It might have been about me."

Cleaver smoothed his moustache again, drawing down the corners of his mouth. "Well," he said, "ain't none of us without a secret of some kind. And Dylan sure was good at rooting out secrets. What you say to him when he tried to shake you down?"

"I said nothing. I haven't got half a million dollars, and if I had I wouldn't have given it to him."

"But you were worried."

"Wouldn't you have been, if Dylan Riley had something on you?"

Cleaver chuckled. "Damn right," he said. "Our deceased friend was a determined and unrelenting man. But not a blackmailer, I would say."

They passed by the fountain again and cut away across the Park. The sky was clouded over now and although the rain had not started in earnest it soon would. They quickened their pace. "How you like the climate here, Mr Glass?" Cleaver asked. "Remind you of the Emerald Isle?" They came to the Tavern on the Green and Cleaver said: "I hear you can get a modest drink of something here for as little as thirty or forty bucks. Want to risk it?"

They went upstairs and sat at a low table and a pretty blonde waitress came and enquired with a singsong lilt what all they would like today. Cleaver asked for a spritzer and Glass said he would have the same.

"You know what this place used to be?" Cleaver said, looking about the dark-timbered room. "A sheepfold. I'm not fooling. There was a flock of sheep here in the Park until the middle of the nineteen thirties, and this was the woolly fellows' fold, until old man Moses — that's Robert Moses the master-builder — ordered them out to Prospect Park. There was a shepherd and all. This city, man, this city." Their drinks arrived and Cleaver lifted his. "Departed friends," he said. They drank the dubious toast and Cleaver leaned back on his seat and contemplated Glass with a mirthful eye. "He was real disappointed in you, you know," he said, with a playful, lopsided grin, "our pal Riley. Thought you were selling out, agreeing to write up your daddy-in-law's adventures."

"So he said. He knew nothing about me."

"Oh, he did, my friend. He knew plenty about you. He made it his business."

"Facts are just facts. You know that as well as I do."

"True, brother, I won't deny it. A fact is a fact is a fact, as the poet said, or something like it. Unless it's a fact that somebody wants to keep us from learning about. You know what I mean?"

Glass could hear the faint susurrus of rain outside. He pictured an antique greensward and sheep at graze; it might have been a scene by Winslow Homer. Surely Cleaver had invented the shepherd of Central Park and his flock. He did not know quite how to take the man, with his gleaming grin and vestigial beard and black-and-white minstrel get-up. He had the distinct, uneasy feeling that this seemingly rambling conversation in which he had become more and more deeply entangled was about everything except what Cleaver really wanted to say, what he wanted to find out, whatever it might be. He asked: "What did you write about Mr Mulholland?"

"In *Slash*? Oh, nothing very terrible. His James Bond days of derring-do, the Mulholland millions and how he made them and what he does with them — that sort of thing."

"And what did you write about the Mulholland Trust?"

Cleaver hesitated, tapping a fingernail against one of his big front teeth. "I know you have a particular interest there, Mr Glass, what with Mrs Glass being the head honcho-ess of the Trust and all. And now her son, Sir Youngblood Sinclair, is taking over the controls, so I hear." He snickered. "My friend," he said, in his Dixieland croon, "you going to find it tough to write dis-passion-ately about all that. Ain't that so?"

He gulped down the last of his drink; Glass had hardly touched his.

"Tell me," Glass said, "tell me who you think killed Dylan Riley."

Cleaver turned on him a stare of mock startlement, making his eyes pop. "Why, if I knew that I'd go straight to Cap'n Ambrose down there at Po-lice Headquarters and tell him, I sure would."

"Do you think my father-in-law had a hand in it?"

"Why would I think that?"

"I don't know. Maybe you think that what Riley found out *was* something about him."

"Maybe it was — you're the one Riley spoke to, he give you no idea at all what kind of secret thing he had uncovered?"

Glass shook his head. "I told you, I thought at first it was something to do with me, but now I'm not so sure."

"You got a secret worth killing for, Mr Glass?" Cleaver grinned teasingly, showing a pointed pink tongue-tip. "You don't seem the violent type, to me."

Glass pushed his drink aside and stood up. "I've got to go. It was interesting talking to you, Mr Cleaver."

80

He offered a handshake but Cleaver ignored it, and sat back on his seat with his legs crossed and jiggled one elegantly shod foot, smiling broadly with his head on one side. "You a cool customer, Glass," he said. "Guy calls you up to stiff you, so you say, and a few hours later he gets a bullet through the eye. You mention to the po-lice about Dylan trying to blackmail you? 'Cause I bet old Cap'n Ambrose would be real interested in that. Don't you think?"

"Goodbye, Cleaver," Glass said.

CHAPTER
NINE

Odalisque

They had been in bed together all afternoon, Glass and his girl, and now at evening he was sprawled pasha-like in his undershorts against a bank of pillows while at her worktable Alison sat, with her back turned towards him, naked, on a red-plush piano stool, before the glowing and intently silent screen of her laptop. Glass was smoking a cigarette. He was happy, or at least content. There was something so sweetly sad about sex in the afternoon. It was raining outside, and the pearly light falling down through the studio apartment's big, slanted window was almost Irish. He only ever felt really homesick when it rained. He was thinking in a dreamy vacancy how much the sound that the computer keyboard made reminded him of his long-dead granny clacking her dentures, and how Alison's shapely back recalled Man Ray's photograph of Kiki de Montparnasse posing as a violin.

"Jesus," she said suddenly, "have you seen this blog?"

"This what?"

"For God's sake, don't pretend you don't know what a blog is."

"Something on the Internet?" He liked to tease her.

She turned to look at him, the rain-light silvering her breasts. "How did you ever manage to be a journalist, with so little experience of the world?"

"The Internet is not the world, my dear."

"Well, *my dear*," she drawled, "everyone in the world uses it, except you."

Her dark hair reached almost to her bare shoulders, making an oval frame for her sharp-chinned, long, pale face. Without her clothes she looked less like a madonna than one of Modigliani's pink-and-platinum odalisques. She had put a towel under her bottom to keep what of him was still inside her from leaking on to the plush of the piano seat. He marvelled how she had managed to shed so comprehensively the Irish squeamishness before the prospect of being. He had grown up expecting that a girl getting out of bed would immediately wrap a sheet round herself, tucking it deftly under her armpits, as girls in the movies always did.

"It's this fellow Cleaver," she said. "The fellow who phoned here for you."

"What?" He was all attention suddenly. "*What* is him?"

"His blog. *Cleaver's Cleaver*, he calls it. 'All the news that's fit to punt.' He's writing about that researcher you were going to hire — Dylan Riley? The one you were asking me about the other day." She read on in silence, then said, "*Jesus*," again. "Did you know he was murdered?"

"Who?"

"This *Riley* person. He was shot. Someone shot and killed him." She turned to him again, almost angrily. "Did you know about this?"

He looked at the ceiling. "Umm."

"Why didn't you tell me? And don't give me some smart answer." She was glaring at him now. "You said he tried to blackmail you. About us."

He sat upright, dashing cigarette ash in the direction of the Betty Boop plastic ashtray he had bought one winter day on a trip he and Alison had made to Coney Island. "I didn't say it was about us. I *thought* it *might* be about us. He claimed to know something, to have found out something, that's all." He did his mime-artist's shrug, lifting high his shoulders and pulling down the corners of his mouth in a show of helplessness. "He wouldn't tell me what it was."

Alison sat without moving, seeming hardly to breathe, watching him steadily. She had gone into her idling mode, waiting for what was to come. Under her blank scrutiny he grew twitchy and irritated, as always. "Look," he said, "I don't know any more about this business than you do. I spoke to Dylan Riley a couple of times, and met him once. The next thing I knew he was dead. Christ knows who killed him. He was a professional busybody, he had a lot of enemies."

Angrily she pushed a strand of hair away from her cheek. "He had it coming to him, is that what you mean?"

"No, that's not what I mean. What do you want me to say?"

"What do I want you to say? Sometimes I think you think you're living in a play, spouting clichés someone else has written for you. I want you to say what you know. I want you to tell me the *truth*."

He climbed off the wide, low mattress — the bed was a bare wood frame resting on four squat pillars of bricks — and strode off to the bathroom. This was a cramped space, not much bigger than a closet, with an angled ceiling and an unshiftable dank smell. He locked the door behind him and sat down on the lavatory lid and held his face in his hands. He felt harried, and almost comically hampered, like a clown who has got something stuck to the sole of his big, floppy shoe and cannot shake it off.

He heard the sound of Alison's impatient barefoot step approaching. "Come on," she said through the door, "don't hide in there."

"I'm not hiding." He stood up, and caught his reflection in the mirror on the wall above the sink. He had a desperate, querulous look, like that of an escaped convict who has heard the first faint baying of bloodhounds in the distance. He put his fingers under his eyes and pulled down the lower lids, making a lizard face. He stuck out his tongue; it had an unpleasant grey coating. For a second he seemed to see, superimposed on his own face, that of Captain Ambrose, dark-skinned and saintly, smiling at him with mournful compassion. "What do you want me to tell you?" he called back over his shoulder.

Alison struck her knuckles angrily on the door. "Stop *saying* that."

"But I don't know what you *expect* me to say!"

He yanked open the door. She was leaning against the jamb, still naked, with her arms folded under her breasts. The hair at her lap was glossy and tightly curled. *How lovely she is*, he thought, with a stab of sorrow, *how lovely*.

She spoke in a low voice, evenly, showing him what an effort she was making to be forbearing and reasonable. "For a start," she said, "tell me what that Cleaver fellow talked to you about."

"He asked if I had spoken to the po-lice."

"He's black?"

"As the ace of spades."

"Don't let them hear you speak like that over here."

"He put on an Uncle Remus act for me, all hominy grits and natural rhythm. It seemed to amuse him."

She was not listening; she was frowning; she was, he could see, worried; he did not know what he could do about that. "And did you?" she asked.

"Did I what?"

"Speak to the police."

"They spoke to me, or one of them did, anyway. A Captain Ambrose. Melancholy type. Wanted to know about the Menendez brothers."

"The *who?*"

"It doesn't matter. He'd read a piece I wrote."

He walked past her, back into the big studio room. It was growing chill as the twilight densed, and voluminous shadows, grey like watered ink, were gathering under the raked ceiling. He always felt that he should duck when he came in here, under all these slants and angles, and the big grimed window leaning over like that gave him the impression of constantly falling backwards very, very slowly. Alison followed after him. "Aren't you cold?" he asked. He wished she would put on her clothes. He had to think carefully here — what should he tell her and, more importantly, what not — and her nakedness was distracting. When he was growing up in Dublin the glimpse of a nipple would set a young boy's gonads going like the tumblers in a fruit machine. "What did Cleaver say, in this blog of his?" he asked.

Alison went and stood at the table and clicked a key on the laptop. "'What did Dylan Riley know,'" she read, "'that someone felt the need to put a bullet through his eye? Riley, a well-known private researcher, was found at his Vandam workshop on Tuesday, slumped lifeless over his MacBook Pro —'"

"He wasn't slumped over anything," Glass said.

"'— with half his brains splattered across the screen, which in the circumstances is surely symbolic of something. As usual, New York's Finest are scratching their heads for a who and a why. Riley's girlfriend Terri' — with an *i* — 'Taylor told police that' yadda yadda yadda. 'The Cleaver is reliably informed — i.e. the cops told us — that Riley's last phone call was to internationally renowned bleeding-heart journo Mr John Glass, who, as unhappy chance would have it, is at present working on a biography — nay, *the* biography — of his daddy-in-law, electronics mogul and former Company spook Mr William "Big Bill" Mulholland. The Cleaver asks: have we stumbled into a wilderness of mirrors here?'" She turned from the screen. Glass was standing by the bed, buttoning his shirt. She crossed to her side of the bed and took a printed silk wrap from the closet and put it on, all the while studying Glass out of a narrowed eye. "What did Cleaver say when you met him?"

He stooped to put on his trousers, lifting a shoulder defensively against her. "Nothing much. He was just fishing for information, looking for a story."

"And *did* he know about" — she made a grimace — "us?"

"Probably. He called you because he thought your number was mine — he got it from Riley, whose filing system seems to have left a lot to be desired."

"Then Riley did know about us."

"Obviously."

She made a brief laughing sound. "You think there's anything *obvious* about any of this?"

He sighed. He felt weary. He wished he had never heard the name Dylan Riley, and silently cursed his contacts who had recommended him. He began to light another cigarette, but Alison said: "Would you mind not? The place reeks already." She never smoked in the studio.

He fitted the cigarette back into the packet, deliberately, resentfully. "Let's go out and eat," he said.

"It's early."

"I'm hungry."

"Don't snap."

"I didn't."

"You did."

This was how it was between them now, so often, the sudden lunge and whip of irritation, followed by a fuming silence. He took a long breath. "Where do you want to go?"

"Where do we ever go?" She pressed a hand to her forehead. "You find a table, I'll get dressed and follow you."

He turned. "Alison."

She looked at him. "Yes?"

"I'm sorry."

She would not look at him. Something like embarrassment, like shame, almost, sat heavily in the space that separated them.

"This fellow getting killed," she said, "do you think it had something to do with your father-in-law?"

"I don't know." He needed that cigarette. "I hope not."

"Have you talked to . . . have you talked to Louise about it?"

"Not really. Louise doesn't take much interest in things like that."

"Like what?"

"Like people she doesn't know getting murdered. Her range of concerns is limited. Her stocks portfolio. Getting a really good table at Masa. The quality of the top-snow at Klosters this year." He could not stop. "The Mulholland Trust. Her son's future. Me getting my comeuppance."

She tightened her lips. "Go and find us a table," she said.

They ate at the little French place round the corner where they went most evenings when they were together, which were not many, and were becoming fewer. He did not know why Alison put up with him — he would not have put with himself. She was lonely, he supposed, as he was, two exiles from a tiny place stranded here amid all this enormity. The image he entertained of America was that of a buffalo standing foursquare with its great head lifted in the direction of old Europe, and him a microbe perched precariously on the tip of the creature's mighty muzzle. Perhaps he should go home, to Ireland; perhaps they should both go home; together, even; perhaps.

After dinner they strolled over to Washington Square. The rain had stopped and there was a fresh, clean fragrance on the night. Glass recalled their meeting here that winter noon before Christmas when they had walked in the glassy air round and round this bare rectangle, under the spectral trees. The time that had elapsed since then seemed far more than a mere four months. "It was at the Washington Square Bookstore here, in 1920," he said, "that the head of the Society for the Prevention of Vice, chap called Sumner, I believe, bought a copy of the *Little Review* with the Gerty MacDowell episode from *Ulysses* in it, and lodged a complaint with the police that led to the trial of the book for obscenity. I bet you didn't know that."

"You're a mine of information," Alison said drily.

The air had softened with the coming of darkness. Glass loved this city at night, the flash and gleam of it, the heavy hum of life going on everywhere, driven, undaunted.

"What will you do," Alison said, "if you find this killing really is somehow connected with Mulholland?"

"I'm not going to *find* any such thing," he said, in almost a snarl, surprised at his own anger. He took a measured breath. "I told you, there must be dozens of people who would have been glad to see the last of Dylan Riley. Why do you automatically think my father-in-law must be involved?"

"Why are you being so defensive?"

He sighed. "I'm not defensive. I'm just tired of being cross-examined."

"You came to me in a panic after Riley phoned you. Have you forgotten? You were terrified he might have found out about you and me. What else were you frightened of, but that he would tell Big Bill Mulholland you were two-timing his daughter?" She linked her arm in his, not out of affection, but sidling close like an assassin, he thought suddenly, positioning herself to drive the dagger all the deeper. "You've always been afraid of him," she said, "of what he could do to you — of what he could take away from you."

He stopped, and made her stop with him. The square of sky above them had a sickly orange cast. He was breathing heavily, a man at bay. "What do you mean, what he could take away from me?"

She did not reply at once, but stood regarding him with a half-smile, regretfully contemptuous, shaking her head slowly from side to side. "Look at you," she said.

"Look what you've become — what they've made of you."

She detached her arm from his then, sadly but firmly relinquishing him, and turned and walked back in the direction of Bleecker Street. He watched her go. Police sirens, two or three of them together, were whooping somewhere close by. He knew he should follow her, the sirens behind him seemed a frantic urging, yet he could not make himself take the first step. She seemed, like so much else, to be receding from him down a long slope that steepened steadily into darkness.

CHAPTER
TEN

Big Bill

Glass stepped out of the elevator into the apartment and his wife came from the shadows quickly, as if to forestall him, and asked in a low voice, sounding tense and cross, where he had been until this hour. The question was rhetorical; she knew where he had been, more or less. She took his arm, much as Alison O'Keeffe had taken it an hour ago, with urgent and unfond intent. "Billuns is here, and he wants to talk to you. He's mad about something, I can tell." Glass said nothing. He might have guessed his father-in-law had arrived. Something happened to an atmosphere when Big Bill Mulholland stepped into it. They walked forward, Louise's high heels making a sharp rapid noise on the parquet that sounded as if she were clicking her tongue. The light in the apartment was muted, no overhead bulbs burning and all the lamps shedding their subdued radiance downwards, as if in deference to the great man's presence.

He was sitting in an armchair in the drawing room, holding aloft a clear crystal goblet with half an inch of brandy in it, gazing into the liquor's amber depths with one eye narrowed and showing off his raptor's profile.

In his late seventies, he was still impossibly handsome, with the head of an athlete of ancient Greece under a great upright plume of undyed dark hair. It was only when he turned that he showed the flaw in his good looks: his eyes, uncannily like those of his grandson, were set much too close together. They gave him, those eyes, the look of being always meanly at work on some extended, crafty and malign calculation. "Ah, John," he said expansively, "here you are, at last." Without rising from the chair he offered Glass a slender, sun-browned, manicured hand. The little finger sported a ruby signet ring; on his other hand, the one holding the brandy glass, he wore a narrow gold wedding band. "We wondered where you'd got to."

Glass shook the firm, dry hand briefly and then went and sat down on the white sofa, facing his father-in-law. He could sense Louise, a hovering presence, somewhere behind him in the dim lamplight. He wondered for a moment if she might be signalling soundlessly to her father. Mulholland regarded him with what seemed a deep affection, smiling and twinkling in that way he had, nodding a little, like a leader on a balcony bestowing a general vague approval upon the gathered masses of his subjects. "Working late, I hope?" he said. "Delving into my racy past? How is the book coming?"

"Slowly, I'm afraid," Glass said, in a neutral tone.

Mulholland seemed unsurprised, and unperturbed. "Well," he said, "I didn't expect you to hurry. Just keep in mind, though, I'm not immortal, no matter what some people might say."

94

"I'm gathering things," Glass said, lifting his hands and moulding an invisible globe between them. "There's a lot of material."

Mulholland was nodding again, the smile forgotten on his tanned, hawk's face. He was thinking of something else, Glass could see it, the tiny polished wheels turning, the levers engaging.

Louise came and sat on the arm of the sofa beside her husband and even laid a hand weightlessly on his shoulder. "He's in the office every day, nine to five," she said, laughing lightly, and a touch unsteadily. Always in her father's presence her voice had an uncertain wobble that she tried to suppress, and that still sparked Glass's waning protective instincts. He put a hand over her hand that was resting on his shoulder. Mulholland looked at them and a hard, sardonic light came into his face. "How is the office?" he asked. "You settled in? Got everything you need?" He took a sip of brandy, swallowed, sniffed. "I wouldn't want to think of you uncomfortable, down there."

"*Up* there," Louise said. "John is scared of the height." Glass swivelled his head to look up at her but she only smiled at him and made a mischievous face.

"That so?" Mulholland said, without interest. "Guess I don't blame you, these days. We didn't know we were building so many standing affronts to the world." He looked into his glass again. "We didn't know a lot of things. After 'eighty-nine we thought we were in for a spell of peace, unaware of what was slouching towards us out of the festering deserts of Arabia. Now we know."

Glass always marvelled at the complacency with which his father-in-law delivered these solemn addresses; he wondered if it was all a tease, a toying with the tolerance of those around him, a test to see if there was a limit to what he would be let away with. Perhaps this was how all the rich and powerful amused themselves, talking banalities in the sure knowledge of being listened to.

"It's fine," Glass said. "There isn't much I need, just space, and quiet."

Mulholland gave him a quick glance, and seemed to suppress a grin. "Good, good," he said. He held out his empty glass to his daughter. "Lou, my dear, you think I could get maybe another tincture of this very special old pale?" She took the goblet from him and walked away soundlessly down the shadowed room, and opened a door and closed it softly behind her; she would be gone for some time, Glass knew; she was adept at reading her father's signals. The old man sat forward in the armchair and set his elbows on his knees and clasped his hands in front of his chin. He wore a dark-grey Savile Row suit and a handmade silk shirt and John Lobb brogues. Glass fancied he could smell his cologne, a rich, woody fragrance. "This fellow Cleaver," Big Bill said, "you know who I mean? One of life's mosquitoes. He's been buzzing around me for years now. I don't like him. I don't like his tactics. Guy like him, he thinks I'm the enemy because I'm rich. He forgets, this country is founded on money. I've done more for his people, the Mulholland Trust has done more, than all the Mellons and the Bill Gateses put together." He chafed his clasped hands, making the knuckles creak. He did not look at Glass when he asked: "And who is this Riley fellow?"

Glass made no movement. "A researcher," he said.

The old man glanced sidelong from under his eyebrows. "You hired him?"

"I spoke to him," Glass said.

"And?"

"And then he got shot."

"I hope you're not going to tell me that the one thing followed from the other?" Mulholland suddenly grinned, showing a hundred thousand dollars' worth of clean, white, even teeth. "Say you're not going to tell me that, son."

"I'm not going to tell you that."

The lamplight formed still pools round their feet, while above them the dimness hung in billows like the roof of a tent.

"See, I've got to know," Mulholland said. "I've got to know if you're in trouble, because, frankly, if you're in trouble then most likely so am I, and so is my family, and I don't like that. I don't like trouble. You understand?" He rose from the chair, without, Glass noted, the slightest effort, and walked to the fireplace and stood there with his hands in his pockets. "Let me tell you a story," he said, "a tale from the bad old days, when I was in the Company." He laughed shortly, and had to cough a little. He had an eerie aspect, standing there with the top half of him in gloom above the lamplight, a truncated man. "There was a friend of mine — personal friend, as well as professional — who managed to get himself on the wrong side of J. Edgar Hoover. Now that, as I'm sure you know, was not a good place to be, J. Edgar being — well, J. Edgar. I'm talking about the sixties, after Kennedy's time. Doesn't matter what it was that my friend — let's call him Mac — doesn't matter what Mac had done to displease that fat old fag. Matter of fact, I thought it was pretty stupid of him, in the circumstances. Hoover was the kingpin then, and the FBI was unassailable." The lamplight was picking out high points in the shadows, the shine on a clock-face, a gleam of polished wood, a spark from Big Bill's ruby ring. "Anyway," he said, "Hoover was real mad at my friend Mac, and decided to bring him down. Now, Mac was pretty high up, you know, at Langley, but that wasn't going to stop J. Edgar. What he did was he organised a sting operation, though that wasn't what we called it in those days." He paused, musing. "Matter of fact, I can't remember what we called it. Memory's going. Anyway. The trap was that Mac was to be at a certain place at a certain time to take delivery of papers, documents, you know, that were supposed to have come from the Russian embassy in Washington. In fact, what was in the package, though Mac didn't know it, was not papers at all but a big stash of money — serious, serious money — and when it was in Mac's hands J. Edgar's people were supposed to jump out of the bushes and nab him for a corrupt agent taking money from a foreign power, *the* foreign power, and our number-one enemy. Anyway, someone in Hoover's office, who liked Mac and didn't like his boss, tipped him off, and Mac just didn't show up at the appointed rendezvous. Okay? So next day Mac, who was pretty sore, as you can imagine, he went down to the Mayflower Hotel where Hoover ate his lunch every day with his constant companion Clyde Tolson. The maître d' stopped Mac at the desk, worried, I guess, by the wild look in his eye, and when Mac told him he wanted to see Hoover — 'J. Edna,' as he called him — the maître d' said he had a standing instruction that Mr Hoover was never to be interrupted while he was eating his cottage cheese and drinking his glass of milk. 'You tell that bastard,' Mac said, 'that unless he gets his fat ass out here this minute I'm going to announce to this restaurant that the boss of the FBI is a skirt-wearing fag.' So Hoover comes bustling out, and Mac accuses him of trying to entrap him. Hoover, of course, denies all knowledge of the sting, and promises he'll set up an investigation right away to find out who was responsible, says he won't rest until he has identified the miscreant, et cetera, et cetera. So. Week later, Mac and his wife are flying down to Mexico in Mac's private Cessna, just the two of them, with Mac piloting. Half an hour out from Houston, out over the Gulf, *kaboom*. Bomb under the pilot's seat. Wreckage strewn over half a square mile of water. Mac's body was found, the wife's never. At the funeral, Hoover was seen to wipe away a tear." He gave another, quick laugh. "No half-measures for our John Edgar."

Glass was fingering the pack of Marlboros in his coat pocket. He heard the door at the end of the room opening softly, and a moment later Louise appeared, carrying a tray with three glasses. Glass wondered if she had been listening outside the door. At times it seemed to him he did not know his wife at all, that she was a stranger who had entered his life sidewise somehow and stayed on. "Sorry it took so long," she said. "John, I brought you a Jameson." She leaned down to each of the men in turn and they took their glasses, then she put the tray on a low table and brought her own drink — Canada Dry with a sliver of lime — and sat beside her husband on the sofa, crossing her legs and smoothing the hem of her dress on her knee.

"We've been talking about J. Edgar Hoover and his wicked ways," her father told her.

"Oh, yes?" she said. Glass could feel her not looking at him. He sipped his whiskey.

"Your father was telling me," he said, "how Hoover arranged the assassination of a CIA man and his wife."

"Who says it was Hoover?" Big Bill said, with a show of innocent surprise. "I told you, he wept at the funeral." He swirled the brandy in its goblet, smiling again with his teeth.

Louise was still smoothing the stuff of her dress with her fingertips. "Billuns is wondering," she said, not looking up, "what it was exactly you said to that man Riley."

The atmosphere in the room had tightened suddenly. From the library they heard the silvery chiming of the Louis Quinze clock that Mulholland had given them for a wedding present.

"I don't remember telling him anything," Glass said. "We spoke on the phone, he came to the office, I said what I was writing, what I needed —"

100

"What you needed?" Mulholland said. He looked suddenly all the more like a bird of prey, sharp-eyed, motionless. "See, that's what I don't understand, John. Why you *needed* to bring in someone else. I gave you this commission because you're family. I told you that at the time, I said, 'John, I want someone I can trust, and I know I can trust you.' Surely you knew that meant *you*, and not some computer nerd along with you?" He turned to his daughter. "Am I making sense, Lou? Am I being unreasonable?" Louise said nothing, and Mulholland answered for her. "No, I don't think I'm being unreasonable. I don't think I'm being unreasonable at all."

For a while now Glass had felt the room forming an angle behind him, the corner into which he was being backed. "I'm sorry," he said. "It would have been no great thing, to hire a researcher. It's normal. Historians do it all the time."

Mulholland opened his little dark eyes as wide as they would go. "But you're not a historian, John," he said, as if explaining something to a child.

"I'm not a biographer, either."

His father-in-law went on gazing at him almost mournfully for a moment, then set down his brandy glass and slapped his palms on his knees and stood up and walked to the fireplace again. "My problem now, you see, John, is how to handle this. We have here what we used to call a fail-int, that is, a failure of intelligence. I don't know what you told Riley, and I don't know what Riley told this Cleaver guy. When you have a fail-int, you've got to do some creative thinking. That's

101

something you could help me with. Because I have to decide how to deal with Mr Wilson Cleaver and his innuendos."

A voice spoke from the depths of the room: "What about special rendition?" They turned and peered, all three, and David Sinclair came strolling out of the shadows, tossing something small and shiny from one palm to the other. He was smiling. "Surely you could arrange a little thing like that, Granddad."

CHAPTER
ELEVEN

Terri with an *i*

In the morning Glass was sitting after breakfast on the little wrought-iron balcony outside the drawing room, savouring in solitude a third cigarette and a fourth cup of coffee, when his stepson reappeared. Glass had to struggle not to show his annoyance. Usually he was the only one who used the balcony, sharing it with rust and spider webs and a few mouldering remnants of last autumn's leaves. Below him was a courtyard — a courtyard, in Manhattan! — and a little garden with ailanthus and silver birch and dogwood, and other green and brown things he did not know the names of. On certain days in all seasons a very old man in a leather apron was to be seen down there, scraping at the gravel with a rake, slow and careful as a Japanese monk. Today the sun was shining weakly, like an invalid venturing out after a long, bedridden winter, but spring had arrived at last, and now and then a silken shimmery something would come sprinting through the trees, silvering the new buds and shivering the window-panes of the apartments opposite and then going suddenly still, like children stopping in the middle of a chasing game. The square of sky above the courtyard was a pale and grainy blue.

Glass thought of Dylan Riley with his eye shot through; there would be no more spring mornings for him.

"So this is where you hide yourself," David Sinclair said.

Although he had his own duplex over by Columbus Circle the young man often spent the night at what he insisted on referring to as his mother's apartment, no doubt imagining that he was thereby neatly excising Glass from the domestic circle. He stood in the open french windows now, smiling down on his stepfather with that particular mixture of mockery and self-satisfaction that never failed to set Glass's teeth on edge and that was so hard to challenge or deflect. This morning he was dressed in cream slacks and a cream silk shirt and two-tone brown-and-cream shoes with perforated toecaps. A cricket sweater with a pale-blue stripe along the neck was draped over his shoulders. He was on his way to a squash game. With his slicked-down hair and those protuberant little black eyes he bore a strong resemblance to a cartoon Cole Porter.

"Good morning," Glass said coldly.

Sinclair laughed, and stepped on to the balcony and edged round the little metal table and sat down on a wrought-iron chair. He crossed one knee on the other and laced his fingers together in his lap and happily contemplated his stepfather, who was still rumpled from sleep, and also a little hung-over from the four or five whiskeys he had drunk sitting alone on the sofa last night after the rest of the household had gone to bed.

"You've certainly upset Granddad," the young man said lightly. "What were you thinking of?"

Below, a flock of lacquered, dark-brown birds came swooping down from somewhere and settled vexatiously among the ailanthus boughs, windmilling their wings and making a raucous, clockwork chattering.

Glass lit another cigarette and put the packet and his lighter on the table before him. "Have you started your new job yet?" he asked, watching the busy birds.

David Sinclair reached out and took Glass's lighter from the table and sat back and began to lob it from hand to hand, as he had done the night before with whatever it was he had been carrying then. "Not yet. Mother isn't quite as ready to relinquish the reins as she likes to pretend. You know how she is." He smiled, arching an eyebrow; his tone and look suggested he did not for a moment believe his stepfather knew how his mother "was" about the presidency of the Mulholland Trust, or about anything much else, for that matter.

"It's a large thing she's doing for you," Glass said heavily. "I hope you realise that. I hope you acknowledge it, too, now and then."

The young man's smile broadened in delight; he loved to irritate his stepfather. He played on Glass's sensibilities with virtuosic skill, tinkling all the right keys and pressing the pedals at just the right intervals.

"But tell me about this Riley business," Sinclair said. "A murder, no less, and practically in the family! Do the police know who did it, or why?"

"I don't know what the police know. They don't tell me."

Sinclair was regarding him with malicious glee. "Are you a suspect?"

"Why would I be?"

"Oh, I don't know. While he was poking around in Billuns's murky world this Riley might have found out something about *you* that you would rather he hadn't. Hmm?"

Glass gazed at him, and drew on his cigarette and turned away and blew a stream of smoke out over the metal balcony-rail with a show of indifference. Once, when he and Louise were not long married, he had hit his stepson. He could not now remember the exact circumstances. He had said something to the boy, reproved him in some way, and David had sworn at him, and before he could stop himself he had struck the little bastard open-handed across the jaw. It had not been a serious blow, but David had never forgiven him for it — understandably, Glass had to admit. He would have liked to hit him again now, not in passion, not in anger, even, but judiciously, flicking out a fist and catching him a quick jab under the eye, or at the side of that fine-boned nose that was so like his mother's, to knock it out of alignment.

"Do you know my father?" Sinclair asked. "*Mister* Sinclair, the pride of Wall Street?" He seemed to find all titles irresistibly funny.

"I've met him," Glass said warily. "I wouldn't say I know him."

106

The young man turned his face aside and looked down into the courtyard where the birds had intensified their ransacking of the birches and the dogwood trees, as if they were trying to shake something out of them. He must have been reading Glass's thoughts, for now he said: "He used to beat my mother." Glass stared. "Didn't she tell you? Oh, not badly. Just a slap or a punch, now and then. I think he was hot-headed" — he turned back — "like you. I tried to intervene once. I was only a kid. I bit his hand and he tried to throw me out the window. We were in the Waldorf Astoria, on the eighteenth floor. He would have done it, too, only the window didn't open. It was the day after Clinton was elected the first time, so I suppose he was feeling sore." He smiled. "He's not a Democrat, as you probably know."

Glass cleared his throat and stood up, the metal legs of his chair scraping on the balcony's concrete floor. "I've got to go," he said. "I have work waiting."

Sinclair was looking up at him, with his insinuating smile, his head on one side. "Of course," he said softly. "Of course you do."

Glass had stepped through the french windows into the drawing room when Sinclair called after him: "Oh, Da-ad?"

"Yes?"

"Here." He held out his hand. "You forgot your lighter."

It was rush-hour, and Glass had trouble finding a taxi. The streets were electric with spring's sudden overnight arrival, and the trees crowding at the edge of the Park looked as if they were preparing to surge over the railings and set off on a march for the East River. Louise had stopped Glass at the elevator to say that she and David and her father were going out to Bridgehampton, and asked if he wanted to come with them. He said perhaps he would, but later; he did not know if he could face being stranded on Long Island and subject to his father-in-law's steely geniality and his stepson's smiling contempt.

In the lobby of Mulholland Tower he was about to show his pass to the electronic eye at the turnstile when Harry on the security desk spoke his name and waved him over. "You got a caller, Mr Glass." Harry pointed. "She been waiting an hour." She was sitting on a bench under the brass wall-plaque with its portrait in relief of Big Bill Mulholland's handsome profile. She looked familiar yet Glass could not say for the moment who she was. She seemed tiny and lost in that great echoing marble space. She wore a crooked skirt and a short, flowered blouse, and a man's rat-coloured raincoat three or four sizes too big for her. He walked across to her, and she stood up hurriedly, fumbling her hands out of the pockets of the raincoat. Her midriff was bare, and she had a metal stud in her navel. "I'm Terri," she said. "Terri Taylor."

"Ah, yes," Glass said, remembering — the Lemur's girlfriend. "Terri with an *i*."

She gave a forlorn, small smile, gnawing her lip at one side. She had freckles and prominent front teeth, and her long straight hair was dyed black, badly. They stood a moment contemplating each other, both equally at a loss. He asked if she would like to come up to his office but she shook her head quickly. Maybe they would go out and get a cup of coffee, then? "Let's just walk," she said. They went into the street. He was about to put a hand under her elbow but thought better of it. She gave a snuffly laugh. "I seem to have done nothing else but walk since . . ." She let her voice trail off.

Playful gusts of wind swooped along the street. A DHL delivery-man, talking rapidly to himself, wheeled a loaded pallet into an open doorway. A dreadlocked derelict in a St Louis Cardinals sweatshirt was arguing with a fat policeman. Beside a storm drain three ragged sparrows were fighting over a lump of bagel as big as themselves. Glass smiled to himself. New York.

"How are you managing?" he asked. He was wondering why she had come to him, what she might want. "It must be tough."

"Oh, I'm all right, I guess," she said. She had wrapped the raincoat tight around herself; it must have been Riley's. She was pigeon-toed, and her legs were bare, and mottled a little, from the cold. "Dylan and I hadn't been together long. Just since Christmas. We met on Christmas Eve, at a party at Wino's." She looked up at him sideways. "You know it, Wino's? Cool place." She nodded, swallowing hard. "Dylan liked it there." Now she sniffed. He hoped she was not going to cry.

"Have you got people here?" he asked. "Family?"

"No. I'm from Des Moines. Des Moines, Iowa?" She laughed. "Insurance capital of the world. You should see

109

it, the buildings, every one of them owned by an insurance company. Jeez."

They sidestepped a jumbo dog turd — must have been a Great Dane, at least, Glass estimated — and arrived at Madison Avenue. He had never got used to the surprise of turning off tranquil little side-streets on to these great boulevards surging with mad-eyed shoppers and herds of taxis and bawling police cars.

"He liked you, you know," Terri Taylor said. "Dylan, I mean — he liked you."

"Did he?" Glass said, trying not to sound incredulous.

"He said you were one of his heroes. He had cuttings of things you wrote, a whole file of them. He was just thrilled you had asked him to work for you — he was like a kid. 'John Glass,' he kept saying, 'just imagine it, John Glass!'"

"I'm glad to hear that." Was he? He was not sure. "I'm flattered."

"That's how he was. He was an *enthusiast*, Mr Glass. A real *enthusiast*."

Glass was recalling the Lemur sprawled in the leather chair in his office that day up there on the thirty-ninth floor, smirking, and working his jaws on an imaginary wad of gum and clawing at the fork of his drooping jeans; women see their men as other men never see them.

"Have you any idea who . . . who might have . . .?"

She shook her head vehemently, pressing her lips so tightly together they went white. "It's crazy," she said. "Just crazy. Who would have wanted to do such a terrible thing? He didn't harm anybody. He was just a big kid, playing his computer games, surfing the web and gathering things." She laughed. "You know my granddad still has the baseball cards he collected when he was a school kid? He has them all there, in a shoebox, under his bed, shows them to anyone who'll listen to him. Baseball cards! I threw my Barbies in the trash can when I was ten."

Glass hesitated. "Any idea," he ventured, the pavement turning to eggshells under his feet, "any idea what sort of things Dylan gathered about *me*?"

They had come to the corner of Forty-fifth. A squat little woman in an outsized fur coat leading a dachshund on a jewelled leash walked forward against a red light and a taxi screeched to a halt and the driver, another Rastafarian — dreadlocks again — lifted his hands from the wheel and threw back his head and laughed furiously, his teeth gleaming. Terri Taylor smiled, watching the scene. "What?" she said, turning to Glass. The light turned to *Walk*, and they walked.

"Only he phoned me, you see," Glass said. "Apparently he had stumbled on something, I don't know what it was, though he seemed to think it was . . . significant."

"What sort of thing?"

"That's the point — I don't know."

She pondered. They were passing by a bookshop, and a man inside turned to the young woman who was with him and pointed at Glass and said something to her, and the young woman gazed out at Glass with blank interest. There were still people who remembered him, from the days, so far off now, when he had been briefly, mildly, famous.

"I thought," Terri Taylor said, "you hired him to do research on your father-in-law, not on you?" She was puzzled; she did not know what he was asking her.

"Yes, I did," Glass said. "Or I sort of did — there was no formal arrangement in place."

"Well, he was working on Mr Mulholland, I know that, he told me so."

"And what did he say?"

She laughed mournfully. "He *didn't* say. He was kind of secretive, you know? Although . . ." She paused, and her steps slowed, and she gazed down at her turned-in feet in their scuffed and patchy black velvet pumps. "He did mention a name."

Glass waited a beat. "Yes?" he said, keeping his voice under control.

"It was someone Mr Mulholland had worked with. What was it? Oo." She scrunched up her face, trying to remember. "Something like 'varicose', like in varicose veins?"

"Varriker," Glass said. "Charles Varriker."

"That's it. Varriker. Funny name. Do you know him?"

"No," Glass said. "He's dead. He died a long time ago."

CHAPTER
TWELVE

The Protestant Pound

There was nothing more Terri Taylor could give John Glass, beyond the name of Charles Varriker, which kept cropping up with interesting regularity. Glass still did not know why Terri had come to him. Perhaps for her he was one of Dylan Riley's touchstones, all of which she had to visit in turn before she could be free to go home to Des Moines. "New York is not my place," she had said, and then smiled ruefully, "not that I really think Des Moines is, either." She seemed less grief-stricken at the death of Dylan Riley than just weary. She was young, and death was too much for her: too bizarre, too baffling, too unreal. He imagined her in ten years' time, married to an insurance executive and living with him and the kids in a frame house in a suburb on the edge of a city where the cornfields began, mile upon mile of them, stretching away in shining, wind-polished waves to the flat horizon.

"You were one of his heroes", she had said to him of Riley. And someone had shot Riley through the eye.

In the afternoon he walked over to Lexington Avenue and Fiftieth to catch the Hampton Jitney. It was one of the not inconsiderable advantages of being married to money that he did not need to pack when he travelled out to the house on Long Island, since everything he might need was already in place for him there, down to toothbrush and pyjamas.

He hated this journey. It was long and tedious and noisy, and he would arrive reeking of exhaust fumes and in a temper. When he had first heard of the Hampton Jitney he had pictured something out of a Frank Capra madcap comedy, a battered old bus with a bulbous front and cardboard suitcases on the roof, and a Marilyn lookalike sitting up front adjusting her lipstick and trying not to snag her stockings on a broken seat-spring. The reality was, inevitably, otherwise. He had expected sea views, at least, given the narrowness of the island, but there was only the flat, featureless road with filling stations and pizza places and the odd undistinguished hamlet. He supposed Bridgehampton itself was handsome, in a *faux*-Founding-Fathers sort of way, and Silver Barn was certainly a fine house, set stop a low, wooded hill with a view down over pitch pine and scrub oak to an ever-shining line of distant sea. Big Bill had built the house for his third and, according to him, present wife, the globe-trotting journalist Nancy Harrison, who had probably spent altogether no more than a few weeks in the place. In the old days Glass had sometimes come across Nancy, in this or that remote corner of the world where they were both covering some small war or non-man-made calamity, and they would have a drink together and laugh about Big Bill and his ways. The shell of the house had originally been an Amish barn that Big Bill had found somewhere in Pennsylvania and bought and had disassembled and carted up plank by plank to Long Island, where it was rebuilt with many additions and refinements. The wood of the walls was the colour of ash and polished like the handle of a spade.

Louise came out to meet him as he was alighting from the taxi at the Colonial-style front door. She was wearing what he thought of as her Jean Seberg outfit: black pedal-pushers, black-and-white-striped matelot top, a short red silk scarf knotted at her throat. Her hair was tied back and she wore no makeup. He did not think he had ever seen his wife inappropriately attired. He could imagine her on the deck of the *Titanic* in green wellies and a Burberry mac and headscarf. Well, he had loved her once, and her elegance and self-possession were not the least of the things he had loved her for.

She laid her fingertips on his shoulders and kissed him with feathery lightness on the cheek. "How was the trip?"

"Hideous, as usual."

"Billuns came out by chopper. You could have come with him."

"For God's sake, Louise. The 'chopper'!"

She stood back and regarded him with tight-lipped reproach, like a mother gazing upon an unbiddable, scallywag son. "We can't all have the luxury of being unconventional," she said. "We're not all" — he could see her trying to stop herself and failing — "ace reporters."

"Oh, Lou, Lou," he said wearily, "let's not start."

The spring that had taken over the city seemed not to have reached this far east yet, and the sky was an unblemished, milk-grey dome, and he could smell rain coming. "We were about to have a drink," Louise said. "I imagine you could do with one?" Glass followed her inside. Although the house was supposed to be theirs now, his and Louise's — her father had made it over to her, for tax reasons, mainly — Glass always felt a visitor here. Yet he could not but be fond of the place, in a distant sort of way. The tranquil atmosphere that reigned within its warmly burnished walls was a legacy of the simple-living people who had hewn and planed these timbers a hundred years ago or more.

They walked through to the wooden veranda at the back, where there were a couple of porch swings with wheat-coloured cushions and a long, low table, much scarred and stamped with the marks of the many dewed-over glasses that had been set down on it through the years, another form of age-rings. Big Bill was there, reclining on one of the swings with his feet on the table and his ankles crossed, reading the *Wall Street Journal*. It always fascinated Glass that rich men actually read the *Journal*; what could it possibly tell them that they did not know already, and in far more intricate and dirty detail? The old man wore chinos and a pale-pink cashmere sweater, and loafers without socks. Even his ankles were tanned. "John!" he said, and folded the newspaper. "How was the journey?"

"He hates the Jitney," Louise said.

"Too bad. Did you take the new one, with those roomy leather seats?"

"I hate that even more than the old one," Glass said.

His father-in-law laughed. "You're like all us Irish," he said. "You love to suffer."

Manuela, the Filipina maid, appeared with a jug of fresh lemonade and three tall glasses. She set the tray on the table and stood back, smoothing her hands down her apron and smiling at the floor. It was a standing joke in the family that Manuela was hopelessly and incurably infatuated with John Glass, who always confused her in his mind with Clara, Louise's maid in Manhattan. He asked her now to bring him a gin and tonic and she nodded mutely and fled. Louise poured lemonade for herself and her father. Glass went and leaned against the wooden rail of the veranda and lit a cigarette. Below him the smooth lawn stretched away to a high bank of oaks that marked the boundary of the garden. From beyond and above the trees came the sounds of mingled talk and spurts of laughter and even, faintly, the tinkling of glasses; Winner the book agent owned the next house up the hill; Winner was famous for his parties. Manuela came back with Glass's drink and scampered off again.

"It says here," Big Bill said, laying a hand on the folded newspaper beside him on the seat, "that Ulster is the next place to watch. Huge economic potential just waiting for the right boost to get it going." He leaned down and twisted his head to read from the page. "'The Protestant pound is set to give the euro a run for its money.' I like that — the Protestant pound!"

"Chasing Catholic credit," Glass said.

Big Bill gave a small nod and a restrained, tolerant smile. "First they'll have to break with the Brits," he said.

Louise, sitting with her glass at the other end of the swing, laughed lightly. "That's been tried, surely?"

Her father shook his head. "British tax law strangles enterprise. That's what you people in the Republic" — he was addressing Glass — "that's what you understood, the need to slash corporation taxes. Now I remember . . ."

Glass sipped his drink and gazed up at the dense wall of budding trees at the end of the lawn. A thing like a tumbril was making its lumbering way slowly through his head; he could almost feel the wheels creaking. Above all states of mind, boredom was the one he went most in fear of. His father-in-law was recounting the oft-told tale of how, twenty-five years before, he had called a secret meeting of Northern Ireland's leaders on the Isle of Man for the purpose of knocking their heads together and making them see sense about the future of their most misfortunate statelet. Now Glass interrupted him. "Did Charles Varriker accompany you on that historic occasion?"

It was Louise and not her father who registered the sharpest surprise. She stared at her husband and for a second it seemed her lower lip trembled. "Why, John," she murmured, as if he had shouted out an obscenity. Her father looked from Glass to her and back again, fumblingly, like a thrown rider struggling to climb back on his horse. His eyes were suddenly baffled and old. "Charlie?" he said. "No, no, Charlie was dead by then.

118

Why are you asking about him?" He turned to his daughter again, querulously. "Why is he asking about Charlie?"

Louise had regained her equilibrium. She ignored her father's question, and set her lemonade glass firmly on the table and rose. "I must talk to Manuela about dinner," she said, and walked away into the house, slowly, deliberately, holding her back very straight, as if to prevent herself from breaking into a run.

Left alone, the two men were silent for a time. Big Bill looked this way and that at the floor round his feet, as though vaguely in search of something he had dropped. Glass lit a cigarette from the stub of the one he had just finished smoking down to the filter. He felt almost queasy, out here over these deeps and headed into darkness, knowing only how little he knew.

"Charlie Varriker," Big Bill said, in a tone at once morose and defensive, "was one of the finest men it's been my privilege to know. He was great because he was good." He looked up at Glass, and there was a fierce light in his face now. "You know what I mean by that? You got any conception of what I mean by that? Goodness is not a quality that's much valued, nowadays. It's become kind of old-fashioned. Charlie was like that, Charlie was old-fashioned. He believed in honour, decency, loyalty to his friends. Just as I was about to be flayed alive he saved my financial skin, and asked no thanks for it. That was Charlie. He was good, and he was great, and I loved him." He stood up, wincing at some twinge, some inner pinch, and looked out across the garden with eyes from which the light

119

had gone, and that seemed glazed-over and opaque now, like window-panes on which frost has begun to form. "Yes," he said, "I loved him."

He turned and walked into the house, following the way his daughter had gone. Glass, still leaning on the wooden rail, smoked the rest of his cigarette then flicked the butt out on to the grass. The faintest of sounds had started up, and now when he looked out into the air he saw that a fine rain had begun to fall.

Louise and he ate dinner alone, waited on with catlike attentiveness by the unspeaking Manuela. They were in the Indian Room. There were Edward Curtis originals on the walls, and Hopi pots stood in rows on custom-built shelving. The rain whispered on the leaded window beside them, and a greenish light suffused this front half of the room. Louise's father was resting, she said. "I wish you hadn't mentioned Charles Varriker. It upsets him to have to recall all that."

"Yes, that was apparent."

She was cutting a steamed asparagus spear into four equal lengths. "What did he say about him — about Charlie?"

"That he loved him."

She gave an odd little laugh. "Loved him?" she said. "He hated him. And feels guilty, of course."

"Why?"

"Why what?"

"Why did he hate him, and why does he feel guilty about him?"

She paused, with knife and fork lifted, and looked at him. "I suppose you think," she said, "in your usual nastyminded journalist's way, that Billuns has something to feel guilty *for*."

"I wish to God you wouldn't call your father by that ridiculous name." She narrowed her eyes in gathering anger but he went quickly on: "You said he feels guilty. Why, if he's *not* guilty in some way?"

"You're Irish," she said. "Are you telling me it's not possible for people to feel guilt even when they're entirely blameless?"

"No one is ever entirely blameless."

"Oh, don't give me that!" she said, her contempt as quick as a slap across the face. "You can do better than that."

"Then tell me why he feels guilty. There must be a reason."

"He feels guilty because he hated Charlie Varriker, and loved him, and because Charlie saved Mulholland Cable from disaster, and because Charlie killed himself. Don't you know *anything* about human beings?"

They sat for a long moment with gazes locked, and then went back to their plates. The day was ending and the green of twilight was intensifying. Manuela came and lit the two tall candles that stood at either end of the table, and went away again.

"Tell me what happened," Glass said to his wife. "Tell me what happened between Varriker and your father."

"Nothing *happened*. They were partners, or at least Charlie thought they were — my father is not the type to be a partner, as I'm sure you're aware. He ran Mulholland Cable like a department of the CIA, on a"

121

— she smiled thinly — "on a need-to-know basis. Which meant no one knew anything beyond their own little area, except Billuns, who knew everything. That was the trouble, that secretiveness, that . . . arrogance. My father treated men as agents, soldiers, fighters — killers, I suppose — but business isn't warfare, or espionage either, whatever people say. When things started to go wrong he didn't know how to make them right. That was why he brought in Charlie Varriker. Because Charlie was charm — oh, pure charm. And Charlie fixed the business, mended it. And then . . ." She stopped, and looked out at the rain and the gathering dusk.

"And then," Glass said, "he killed himself."

"Yes," his father-in-law said from the doorway, where he had entered unnoticed by either of them. "That's what he did." He came forward into the candlelight and the greenish glow from the window. His face was drawn and grey. "The Goddamned fool took my Beretta and shot himself" — he lifted a finger and pointed — "right here, through the eye."

CHAPTER
THIRTEEN

Some Like It Hot

By morning the rain had cleared, and the vast blue sky was so pale it was almost white. John Glass sat on the pitch-pine veranda with his coffee and his cigarettes and watched the sunlight stealthily leaching the night's shadows out of the trees. He had slept badly and woken at dawn. He had sat first in the big central living room and tried to read, but the silent house with other people asleep in it made him uneasy and so he had come out here. The salt air was cold still. Birds swooped down swiftly to the lawn in pursuit of the early worm and then flew up again.

He was wondering at what time Captain Ambrose started work. He needed to talk to the policeman; there were questions he needed to ask him. He had been wrong about Dylan Riley, all wrong. He had a sense of smouldering anger that at any moment might flare into flame.

Later, he was eating a silent breakfast with Louise in the big sun-filled kitchen when David Sinclair arrived from the city. His mother rose from the table and kissed him, and then held him for a moment at arm's length, scanning his face and touching him lightly here and there with her fingertips, as if to check him for damage. She worried about the places David frequented, the Chelsea clubs and dives where he spent most of his nights. "I know so little of what he does," she would say. "He won't tell me anything." Glass had no comment to make; this was territory he did not venture into willingly.

"*Uh*-oh," David said now, lifting his head and pretending to sniff the air. "This atmosphere that I'm getting. Have you two been having a long day's journey into night? I can almost hear the foghorns." He was wearing a blazer with brass buttons and a crest on the pocket, and white duck trousers and an open-necked white shirt and a Liberty cravat. All he lacked was a yachting cap. The young man had as many personalities as he had outfits. And he had seen too many movies. Today he was Tony Curtis in *Some Like It Hot*, camp lisp and all. When his mother asked how he had managed to arrive so early he said he had driven up, setting out at six while the dawn was still an hour off. "They say the city never sleeps," he said, "but it does, it does. There wasn't a soul about, not even a bag-lady." He turned suddenly to Glass. "Anybody else get shot since I saw you last?"

Big Bill appeared then, unshaven, in a terrycloth robe and purple velvet slippers. He looked greatly unwell. The tanned skin of his cheeks still had a greyish tinge, and the stubble on his chin glittered like spilled grains of salt. After her father had gone to bed the night before Louise had berated her husband yet again for bringing up the painful subject of Charles Varriker and his suicide. "Don't you think he deserves a bit of peace," she had said, "after all these years?" Peace, Glass thought, did not come into it; peace was not the point.

"Good morning, *Granddad*," David Sinclair said, with exaggerated deference.

Big Bill gave him a sliding glance from under his eyebrows and muttered something and sat down at the table. Glass wondered how Louise had persuaded her father to let her hand over the directorship of the Mulholland Trust to a young man who was the old man's opposite in every way imaginable. Would he understand it, he wondered, if he had a daughter who herself had a son? The subtleties of familial loves and loyalties baffled him; his own father had died too young.

Big Bill drank the coffee that Louise had poured for him and crumbled a piece of bread in his fingers but did not eat it. Glass noticed the tremor in his hand. He had aged overnight. "Need someone to drive me down to St Andrew's," he said. St Andrew's in Sag Harbor was where he heard Mass on Sundays when he was at Silver Barn.

"You can do that, can't you, darling?" Louise said to her son.

"But of course," David said, with fake eagerness, and turned to his grandfather. "I'll come to Mass, too. Simply can't resist those gorgeous vestments."

He winked at Glass. Big Bill said nothing.

In the end all four of them climbed into David Sinclair's vintage open-top gold Mercedes, the old man

125

in the passenger seat and Glass and Louise crowded together in the back. As they drew away from the house and set off down the hill Glass realised he had forgotten to call Captain Ambrose. Was he afraid of what the policeman might have to tell him? And would it be any more than he suspected, any more than he dreaded? Without wanting to he knew now, he was sure of it, who had shot Dylan Riley. Or who had arranged for him to be shot.

At the church it was apparent that Big Bill expected them to accompany him inside, but Glass said he would take a walk down by the water, and insisted that Louise should come with him. The old man grunted and turned abruptly and set off across the street to the church. David looked at his mother and smiled enquiringly. "Go on," she said, "go with him. He'll be pleased."

There were not many people at the harbour, the season proper not having begun yet. They walked out on to the Long Wharf. The water swayed and wallowed, sluggish as oil in the calm of morning. Across the bay the low hills on Shelter Island, where the last of winter seemed to linger still, were a surly olive-green. The sharp air, reeking of iodine and salt, stung their nostrils.

"Tell me about Charles Varriker," Glass said.

Louise was wearing knee-high black leather boots and a tweed cape over a heavy Aran sweater. She walked with her arms tightly folded against the chill of morning. She was pale, and her eyes had a faintly haunted look. He suspected she, too, had passed a sleepless night. He wondered what she was thinking now; he always wondered what she was thinking.

"Tell you what?" she said. "What can I tell you, that I haven't already?"

"Why did he kill himself?"

"Why does anybody? No one ever knows."

"Did he leave a note?"

"Of course not." She stopped, and turned to him. "Why are you so interested in this?"

"Dylan Riley found out something, something I thought at first had to do with me but now I think had to do with Varriker. And before you ask, I don't know what it was."

They walked on.

"I wish," Louise said, "that you'd start being a journalist again. You need something to occupy you."

"That's what the priests used to tell us — an idle mind is the devil's workshop. Good title for a book, don't you think? *The Devil's Workshop*. Maybe that's what I'll call Big Bill's biography."

"That's not funny."

"I thought it was."

"You love to needle me, don't you? It's a kind of hobby for you."

A little white sailing boat with sails furled and its outboard going came weaving through the throngs of millionaires' yachts, cleaving a clean furrow in the water that, close in here, had a milky shine like the inner lining of an oyster shell. A whiskery fellow in a sailor's cap and faded blue sailcloth trousers rolled to the knee stood in the prow with one bare foot planted on the topmost strake. It amused Glass that everyone here dressed the part, like hopeful extras waiting for the camera crew to arrive.

They came to a little restaurant adorned with knotted ropes and red-and-white lifebuoys and festoons of fishing-net. They took an outside table from where they could watch the Old Man of the Sea tying up his boat to a post of rough-hewn timber. A buxom girl with a big toothy smile came and took their order. Louise sat low in her chair with her hands clasped under her cape and her booted legs thrust out before her, crossed at the ankles. "I don't want to talk to you about Charlie Varriker," she said.

"Then I'll ask your father." He waited, and she said nothing. "There's something not right here, Lou. And it's to do with Varriker, I'm sure of it. I don't know how, but I'm sure."

"Since when," she flashed at him, "did you start to care again about things not being right?" She continued glaring for a moment, then turned aside with her lips pursed and her eyes narrowed. "Charlie was a good man," she said. "He didn't deserve to die. *That* wasn't right."

"Dylan Riley didn't deserve to die either."

"Oh, yes?" she said, and gave him a sardonic look. "And you're going to avenge his death, are you?"

"I want to know for certain who killed him. Maybe I've decided to be a journalist again, as you say I should." He waited, then said: "What happened, with Charlie Varriker? Tell me, Lou."

The old sailor, squatting on his heels, was fashioning an elaborate knot in the boat's painter. He had lit a cigarette and stuck it in the corner of his mouth, from where a line of smoke ran straight up into his left eye. He knew, Glass saw, that Louise was watching him; male vanity never ages.

The girl brought their coffee.

"Charlie was Billuns's best recruit," Louise said.

"At the CIA?"

She ignored the question as too obvious to require an answer. "Billuns was so proud of him. God knows the things he had got him to do — there had been some 'op', as they used to say, in Vietnam that Charlie would never talk about, that had been a great success, just before the Tet Offensive. They used to get drunk together and make toasts to Ho Chi Minh and General Giap. They were like schoolboys, or like a schoolboy and his teacher." She stopped.

"And?"

Louise sipped her coffee and grimaced. "It's hot," she said, "be careful." The old sailor had gone. A family of five fatties waddled past, making the wharf groan under them. The three roly-poly children wore identical, brand-new Sag Harbor tee-shirts. One of them, a girl, had an exquisitely pretty face encased in a football of fat. Louise resumed her cheerless sprawl, shoving her hands into the sleeves of her sweater. "And nothing," she said. "Billuns brought in Charlie to fix whatever it was that had gone wrong at Mulholland Cable, and he did, he fixed it. He could fix anything, with that way of his. And then he killed himself." She was looking out at the drab green hills across the bay, her eyes narrowed again and her mouth making tiny movements behind tightened lips as if she were biting on something small and hard between her teeth.

"How well did you know him?" Glass asked.

"Who — Charlie? He was Billuns's employee, then his partner, then he was dead. People came and went like that, in our life, in those days. It was a hectic time Things changed from one day to the next. Someone was there and then gone. That was the kind of world it was."

"And you hated it." Only when he had said it did it strike him as surely true.

"What was there to hate?" she said, on a suddenly weary note. "It was my life. It was what I knew. There was no changing that."

"You mean," he said, "there was no escaping it?"

She smiled, for what seemed to him the first time in a long time. "*You* were supposed to be my escape," she said.

"What about Mr Sinclair?"

"Oh, he was just" — she waved a hand, again in seeming weariness — "he was just someone along the way."

"Along the way to *me*?"

"Just — along the way."

The sun's faint warmth was lifting a tarry smell from the wooden table-top between them.

"I'm sorry," Glass said, not knowing exactly what it was he was sorry for.

To his surprise, she reached out and touched the back of his hand with her fingertips. "Don't be," she said. "I'm not. Not really." Then she pushed her coffee cup aside and stood up, pulling the heavy cape close about her. "Brr," she said, "I'm cold. Let's go — Mass will be over by now."

When they got back to the church Big Bill and his grandson were already in the car. Sitting upright there, the top half of Big Bill looked like a ruined monument to some immemorial chieftain, his eagle's profile and dark crest of hair suggesting a warrior race, long extinct. "I told you you had upset him," Louise murmured.

David Sinclair saw them and waved. "We had a wonderful sermon, very edifying," he said. "Mammon and the media and the craze for celebrity. How modern the priesthood has become all of a sudden. Not so long ago it was hellfire and the hope of salvation. What happened to good old-timey religion, that's what I want to know."

His grandfather sat motionless, seeming not to hear him. When he blinked, his eyelids fell like miniature canvas flaps. They drove back up to the house in silence except for Sinclair's happy humming. As they travelled inland the salt-sea smell gave way to scents of grass and pine. In the back seat Glass tried to catch his wife's eye but she looked out steadily at the road, her hair shaking in the wind.

Manuela had set out drinks in the drawing room, lemonade, her specialty, and herb tea for Big Bill and Louise, and Glass's habitual gin and ice and lemon and tonic water. But Glass did not feel like drinking, and walked out to the veranda and smoked a cigarette instead. The birds, quieter now, browsed among the trees, whistling and chattering. Presently David Sinclair came out, carrying a tall tumbler of lemonade. Glass ignored him, hoping he would go away, but the young man instead sat down on one of the swings and began happily rocking himself forward and back, his feet lifted free of the floor. "They're planning a pow-wow on my future," he said. "Mother and Billuns, that is. I'm supposed to join them, but really, I can't face it." He smiled, compressing his lips, which were so pink they might have been painted. "You don't believe in all this for one little moment, do you? I mean me as pontiff of the one, holy and apostolic Mulholland Trust."

"I believe," Glass said, "that the Trust does good work."

"Oh, yes," David said, heaving a histrionic sigh. "That's what makes it so boring."

Glass heard himself breathing, as he always did when he was angry. He threw away his cigarette and turned aside, muttering something, and walked into the house, and up to his bedroom, and shut the door behind him and sat on the side of the bed and picked up the telephone and dialled, and after a moment said: "Captain Ambrose, is he there? I'd like to speak to him. Glass, tell him. John Glass."

CHAPTER
FOURTEEN

The Love-Nest

When Glass arrived at his office next morning there was a message waiting on the answering machine. It was from Terri Taylor, to say goodbye. Her father had come in from Des Moines and she was flying back with him — "Going home to Insurance Land," as she said, with one of her snuffly, apologetic little laughs. The machine made her voice sound hollow and distant, as if she were speaking already from way out on those far plains. He found, to his surprise, that he was touched she should have thought to call him, but then he reflected that perhaps she had no one else in New York to say goodbye to.

He sat down at his desk. He had expected there would be a message from Alison O'Keeffe. He thought of calling her, and even picked up the phone, but set it back again, slowly, in its notch. And immediately the thing rang.

"Wilson Cleaver here. How you doing, brother?" Cleaver sounded chirpy and amused, as usual, enjoying immensely his ongoing private joke at the world's expense. "What's the news, Sherlock? You catch the dastardly culprit yet who gave our nosy friend one in the eye?"

"No. But I think I know who it was."

That brought a silence on the line. Cleaver breathed for a while, thinking, and then said: "You care to say a name?" More silence. "No, I guess not."

"I want to talk to you. About Charles Varriker."

"Heh, heh. Now where'd I hear that name before?"

They met at an Irish bar on Broadway. The bar was Cleaver's suggestion, another detail added to the big joke's already crowded scenario. Muldoon's was a great dim barn of a place, with tricolours on the walls and shamrocks everywhere, and framed parchments with droll Irish verses graven in curlicued script, and a muscular bar girl in an outfit of black felt and bits of white lace that might have been worn by a Welsh milkmaid in a time of myth. Cleaver today wore jeans and a leather jacket and scuffed sneakers, an outfit in which he looked almost ordinary. He ordered a pint of Guinness, and Glass asked for a Jameson, despite the early hour. "Varriker," he said. "What do you know about him?"

Cleaver did his eye-widening act. "Man, you the one with all the knowledge — you tell me."

"When we had that drink, at the Tavern on the Green, you knew a lot of things about him. You even knew what day of the week he died on. What got you so interested in him that you made it your business to find out all that?"

Cleaver showed his dusty-pink palms. "I told you, I was reading up on Big Bill Mulholland. A lot of facts fell out. You know how it is."

"Useless facts, or otherwise?"

Cleaver dipped a prehensile upper lip into the creamy froth of his Guinness and sucked up a wedge of the shiny, ebony-coloured stout. "Jesus," he said, grimacing, "how do you guys drink this stuff?"

Glass indicated his shot-glass. "I don't."

"You don't drink Guinness? What kind of an Irishman are you, brother? You ain't even got red hair."

The brawny barmaid hovered near them, eavesdropping on their talk while pretending to be polishing the counter top.

"Listen," Glass said, "I think Varriker is the key to everything."

Cleaver gave him an exaggerated stare, still playing at being Mister Bones. There were tiny red striations all over the slightly yellowish whites of his eyes. "'Everything' being Dylan Riley getting whacked? How come?"

"I don't know." Cleaver took this in, sucking his teeth at one side and slowly nodding. "What do you know about Varriker's death?" Glass asked. "Where was he when he died?"

"Place up near Harlem. Had a room in an apartment house there, pretty run-down. Sounded like a love-nest, to my suspicious way of thinking. Left no note, nothing. And all the time that first-class ticket to gay Paree was waiting for him at an Amex office over there on Lexington. Course, people do the darnedest things on the spur of the moment, even down to shooting their brains out."

Glass was looking into his whiskey. "Do you know how he was shot?" he asked. Cleaver said nothing.

"Through the eye, with a Beretta. Just like Dylan Riley. Now *that*, my friend, *that* is a coincidence." He left his untouched drink on the bar and stood. "And if it's not," he asked, "then what is it?"

Cleaver followed him into the street. They stood together for a moment, unsure how to part. The day glared unreally, in a parody of April weather, the sunlight glancing in spikes off car roofs and shop windows. A fat mauve cloud with an edge of burning magnesium was elbowing its way up the narrow strip of sky above Fifth Avenue.

"You know," Cleaver said, "that blackmail stuff with Riley. It wasn't real. He didn't care about money. It was *you* he cared about, what he thought you were doing to yourself." Glass said nothing. He knew it was true, so what was there to say? Cleaver smiled. "You look to me," he said, "like a man about to cause an awful lot of trouble." He had at last let drop the black-and-white-minstrel act. "Do I need to urge you to take it easy, to watch your back?"

Glass was squinting up at the advancing raincloud. "I want you to do something for me," he said.

"Anything for a comrade."

"If nothing comes of this — if I get nowhere — if I'm stopped, and you hear no more of all this, don't let it go. Keep digging, and publish what you turn up. Don't worry about Mulholland or what he can do. Just keep on."

Cleaver was half smiling, with eyebrows lifted and his head held on one side. "That's what we do, my friend," he said. "We keep on." He offered a hand. "Good luck."

136

When, half an hour later, Glass got to the apartment overlooking the Park there were shadows standing like transparent pillars in the high rooms. The cloud over the city had released its rain and moved on, and the sun was in the streets again, but indoors a wistful dimness persisted, vague as memory. Glass moved through a silence that seemed to cling like gauze. "All hands," he murmured, his usual greeting, but with no one to hear.

In the library he found his father-in-law sitting in the middle of the white sofa, straight-backed as always, with head erect, in the pose of a tribal elder, his big, liver-spotted hands set on his knees and his feet in their handmade brogues planted side by side on the polished parquet. Glass wished that he could just turn now and walk away, away to a time before the Lemur had come to his office, before Captain Ambrose had called him, before he had met Cleaver, before anyone had died.

The old man started, and looked at him, keeping his head set forward and only swivelling his eyes sideways. "What do you want?" he asked.

Glass sat down opposite him on a delicate Regency chair with a striped silk seat and curved legs ending in lion's claws. "I want," he said, "to know the truth about Charles Varriker."

The old man gave a phlegmy laugh. "It's my life story you're supposed to be writing, not Charlie Varriker's."

"You hated him. Why?"

He shrugged. "What if I did? He was good, but just *too* damned good. That was supposed to be *my* thing. *I* was the one who was virtuous despite all the odds. But

137

Charlie was better. Charlie was truly a virtuous man. It was unnatural. And it grated on me."

"And therefore he had to die."

Big Bill had stopped listening, and was looking about distractedly. "You think you could fix me a drink?" he asked. "I really need a drink."

Faintly, from the hallway, Glass heard the whirr of the elevator as it came to life; someone had called it. He went into the dining room and poured a go of Bushmills whiskey over a glass of ice and brought it back to the library and handed it to his father-in-law. The old man held the glass in both hands and drank greedily, the ice cubes knocking, then leaned back against the sofa wiping at his lips with his fingertips. "What did you say about Charlie's death?" he asked. "All I know is it was a crime and a sin, and I don't forgive him for it."

"Did you kill him?" Glass asked.

For a moment it seemed that Big Bill had not heard. Then he turned his weary eyes again and looked at his son-in-law for a long moment, expressionless. "What are you talking about, you stupid son of a bitch?" he said at last, softly. "Kill him? Why would I kill him?"

"I don't know. Because you hated him."

"He killed *himself*, for Christ's sake. He shot himself through the Goddamned eye, with my gun — I told you."

"Yes, I know you did. But that's how Dylan Riley was shot, too. With a Beretta. Through the eye."

"What?" The old man was shaking his head. "I don't understand — what do you mean?"

138

The lift was whirring again, and there was the faint clatter of it rising. Glass had been wondering where Clara the maid could be — perhaps this was she, coming back from the store.

"Dylan Riley," Glass said, "the researcher I hired to work for me. He was shot in just the same way that Varriker was, through the eye, with a Beretta. I think you did it. I think you shot Varriker, and Riley found out somehow, and then you had to shoot him, too. Or maybe you had it done — maybe you called in a favour from your old friends in the Company. Is that what happened?"

When Louise and her son came into the room Glass experienced a moment of incongruous pure flashback to his boyhood, when he and his own mother on some unremembered afternoon must have entered a room somewhere in just this way, carrying packages and talking together and bringing with them the cool air of outdoors, with all its spring fragrances of trees in leaf and rained-on pavements, the delicate, drenched, petrol-blue air of April. He closed his eyes for a second. Why should he not just shut up now, claw back what had already been said — Big Bill seemed lost in bewilderment — and let the whole thing go, forget what he thought he knew, leave the dead to their own devices. If he kept on the would destroy the world that he and Louise had worked so long and hard to hold intact, to smash the elaborate jewel box that both contained and supplied adornment for his life. Was that what he really wanted?

Big Bill stood up lumberingly, half the whiskey in his glass splashing on the carpet. "Lou," he said, in a loud, whining voice, as if she were much farther away from him than she was, "you know what this guy is accusing me of?" He turned his furious, narrow glare on his son-in-law. "You tell her!"

Louise had stopped motionless in the middle of the floor. She was wearing a little green coat tightly belted at the waist and her spun-sugar Philip Treacy hat. Her face had gone as pale as paper. She looked quickly from her father to Glass and back again, scanning, assessing, calculating. David Sinclair, resembling today a sleek young priest, in a black silk suit and white polo-neck, took the shopping packages from her hands and set them with his own on a low table by the fireplace and turned back, smiling eagerly, avid for whatever might be coming next.

"Dylan Riley telephoned me on the day he was murdered," Glass said, looking at none of them but conscious of their eyes on him. He could hear himself breathing, *hiss*-hiss. *hiss*-hiss. "He phoned twice, in fact. Only one of those calls reached me, in the office. The second time he called, he called here." It was what he had remembered Captain Ambrose saying, that Riley's phone had logged two telephone calls to him; what Ambrose had omitted to say, until Glass phoned him yesterday from Bridgehampton, was that the two calls had been made to different numbers, one at the office in Mulholland Tower, and the other here at the apartment. "What I'm wondering is, who took the second call?"

Mulholland lumbered a step forward until he was looming over his son-in-law. The knuckles of his hand that held the whiskey glass were white under the suntan. He swayed a little. "What are you trying to do here?" he asked, almost plaintively. "What kind of mischief are you trying to make?"

Glass lit a cigarette with a hand that shook.

"He's saying," David Sinclair said, still smiling, his eyes a-glitter, "that a person in this room shot Dylan Riley — only he has the wrong person."

"David!" Louise cried, and it was as if something had propelled itself out of her, a tangible fragment of woe, and then, "*David*," she said again, softly. "Stop, please stop."

Her son ignored her. He looked at Glass and his smile became almost tender. "But it's true, isn't it, Monsieur Poirot?" He stood with his hands lightly in the pockets of his jacket, his thumbs hooked on the outside, in the pose of an English royal. A knotted nerve was twitching at one side of his mouth. Big Bill gave a sort of groan, twisting up his lips as if at some awful taste, and set the tumbler down with a thud on the little table where the parcels were stacked. "This is crazy," he said. "I don't understand this." He turned abruptly and shambled off, shaking his head and muttering under his breath. Louise spoke his name but he waved a hand behind him, shooing away her appeal in angry dismissiveness, and went on. At the door he paused for a moment, still with his back turned to the room, his head lowered, then softly he opened the door and went out and as softly shut it behind him again.

"Well well," David Sinclair said into the silence of his grandfather's departure, "and then there were three!"

Louise, as if coming suddenly out of a trance, put a hand to her forehead and shut her eyes briefly. "This is," she said, "this is . . ." and could not finish. She opened her eyes and looked at her husband. "Why are you *doing* this? You don't *need* to, you don't need to . . . to . . ."

"*Need?*" Glass said. "Where does *need* come into it?"

"He doesn't understand," David said to his mother, as if to soothe her. "He's just an old broken-down reporter who's missed the story entirely." He smiled again at Glass. "Haven't you? Because you see, *Dad*, it's *Murder on the Orient Express*. We *all* did it, all of us — including you."

CHAPTER
FIFTEEN

All in the Family

Throughout his life, so it seemed, John Glass had been running to women for solace. People had remarked when he was young on his closeness to his mother — one of his aunts used to say, with a sour little sniff, that he was more like her boyfriend than her son. Louise, too, he had looked to for reassurance and protection. He suspected it was mainly this that he had married her for, to be his shield against the world's buffetings. And she, what had she hoped for from him?

When he stopped on Bleecker Street and pressed the doorbell the intercom did its rattle and squawk and then Alison O'Keeffe answered. He spoke his name. "How did I know it would be you?" she said, with rueful weariness. "How did I know that?"

Huddled in the doorway, misting the metal grille with his breath, Glass was reminded of sweaty sessions in the confession box, long ago. He said: "I need to talk to you."

Another pause. "Well, you'd better come up, then."

When he stepped out of the elevator she was waiting in the doorway in her painter's dark-blue smock. She led him upstairs to the little cold apartment, where she sat down in an armchair and lit a Gauloise. She blew an angry-seeming trumpet of smoke at the ceiling. "Well?" she said. "What is it you need to talk about so urgently?"

The sun of late afternoon shone in the mansard window above them, setting a beam of pale-gold light to stand at a slant behind her chair. He lit one of his Marlboros.

"Do you know anything about quantum physics?" he asked. She said nothing. "Neither do I, or not much, anyway. But there's an experiment scientists do, when they fire an atomic particle at a surface with two narrow slits in it, and wait for what will happen on the other side. What happens is that an interference pattern forms, as if the particle was not a particle but a wave. In other words, the single particle seems to go through both slits at the same time, and" — he laughed — "interfere with itself!" Alison watched him impassively. Billows of pale-blue smoke from their cigarettes rolled and tumbled together in the sunlight behind her. "That's strange enough," he said, "but what's stranger still is that the particle only behaves like that, like a wave, *when it's not being observed*. When you're looking at the particle it stays a particle, and when you're not looking it becomes a wave."

She waited. He drew on his cigarette, glancing vaguely here and there about the room and frowning. She asked: "What are you talking about?"

"I'm talking about how hard it is to know anything for certain. I thought I knew who killed Dylan Riley, but I didn't."

A lengthy silence passed, then Alison gave a sort of laugh. "And *I* thought you had come here to talk about us." She turned her eyes aside angrily. "So tell me," she said, "who *did* kill him?"

"It doesn't matter. I was wrong." He looked around for a place to stub out his cigarette. "I should go."

"Yes," she said, her face still turned away from him. "You should."

He walked the streets for a long time, as the day died and the million lights of Manhattan began to come on. He had never felt such a stranger to the city. He ducked into a dive on Broadway and drank whiskey, slumped at the bar in the amber and pink gloom surrounded by indistinct figures like himself, whose faces would materialise for a moment when they leaned down into the harsh white glare coming up from the strip-lighting under the rim of the bar to take a sip from their glasses and then retire back into the shadows. After the third shot he dropped a twenty-dollar bill on the bar and hustled himself out into the night again.

When he got out of the elevator at his floor in Mulholland Tower he would not let himself look out of the big window at the end of the corridor, but inside his office, with its wall of glass, there was no avoiding the vertiginous city out there bristling on its stilts, sleekly bejewelled in the shining darkness. There was no avoiding Louise, either, sitting silently in the steel and leather chair where Dylan Riley had slouched that first day, when all that was to happen had not happened yet, and the world was different. She had not switched on a light, and in the gloaming she might have been a statue fashioned from steel, sharp-featured, burnished, unmoving.

"The night man on the desk let me in," she said. "I hope you don't mind."

He was smoking a cigarette — he had lit it in the elevator, defying the smoke alarm, which anyway had failed to go off — and now he groped on the desk for an ashtray that was not there. He had to search for the switch of the desk lamp, too. It cast a cone of light downwards, its penumbra illuminating the side of Louise's face, an ear, an eye, a corner of her mouth.

"How long have you been here?" he asked.

"Oh, not long." They were like two travellers stranded in a waiting room, at night, far from home. "I guessed this is where you'd be."

She still wore her little green coat and ridiculous hat. Her hands were in her lap. She gazed straight before her. Glass walked to the window and looked out into those dark canyons that at night were less alarming than by day, inexplicably. "I don't know what to say to you, Louise," he said.

He heard her stirring behind him, shifting in the chair, repositioning herself. "You mustn't believe . . ." she began, and stopped. "You mustn't believe the things you think you know. Really, you've mistaken it all." She turned to look at him where he stood with his back to her, and the chair made its little protesting squeak. "Please," she said, "come and sit down."

Distantly from the streets below he heard the wailing and yapping of a police siren, and squinting down he saw it, not the car but only the pulsing blue light speeding along Forty-fourth Street. He turned and walked to the desk and sat, hunching his shoulders and leaning forward on his elbows. He had been tipping the ash of his cigarette into his palm, and now, impatient suddenly, he dropped it on to the floor beside his chair. Louise continued to sit sideways-on to him, showing him her sculpted, lamplit profile. He thought of Alison O'Keeffe sitting like this earlier: two women, their faces set against him.

"I have things to tell you," Louise said, "things I should have told you long ago." She looked down. "I don't know where to begin. Charlie — Charlie Varriker . . ." She stopped.

"You were in love with him," Glass said, "weren't you?"

She nodded, pressing her lips together and closing her eyes. "Yes." She spoke so softly it seemed a kind of distressful sighing. "He was — oh, I can't tell you what he was. I mean I can't explain it. He was . . . everything." She looked down again; she was pulling spasmodically at one of her fingers, as if trying to pull off it a ring that was not there. "I was young, of course — my God, what was I? Twenty-two? And Charlie was — oh, he was just so beautiful. It's not a thing men are supposed to possess, that kind of beauty, but he had it. It wasn't so much a matter of looks, you know, but something that came out from inside, that just — that just *shone out*. And he was funny. It's a cliché, I know, that women will love a man who can make them laugh. But laughter with Charlie was something — something *blessèd*. That will amuse you, I know. I can hear how ridiculous it sounds. But that's what it was, blessèd. 'You know, Lou,' he used to say, 'not once anywhere in the Gospels does Jesus laugh, or even smile. Who could believe in a God that doesn't laugh?'" Glass took another cigarette. "He rented a room for us, in one of those little streets around Morningside Park. What a neighbourhood! We were lucky we weren't murdered for our shoes. It's strange, but somehow the squalor made what we had seem all the more tender, all the more pure. Does that make sense? And then" — she was suddenly in a rush, the words tumbling out — "and then there was the baby, I didn't know what to do, I was too young, and Charlie, of course, Charlie was helpless, so happy and loving and yet helpless, helpless. Rubin had been hanging around — Rubin Sinclair, I mean, Daddy Warbucks, as Charlie used to call him — and Billuns, of course, was insisting I must marry him, I think he saw it as something like a Medici marriage, the melding of two great families blah blah blah. I said to Charlie, 'It's the obvious way out, I'll marry Rubin and after a little while you and I can be together again, we can even have the baby for ourselves.' What a dream. What a fool. Charlie wouldn't hear of it. He couldn't bear to think of me with Rubin, he said, it would kill him, he would die —"

"Why didn't you marry him?" Glass asked.

She made an impatient gesture. "Don't be absurd. Billuns would have destroyed us. He hated Charlie for saving his millions. What do you think he would have felt if he had married his daughter?" She was silent for a moment, picking intently at a loose thread in the seam of her coat. "I bought him a ticket to Paris. Charlie loved Paris, he always said it was his spiritual home. 'Go there,' I told him, 'go to Paris, and when you come back it will be done. That way it won't hurt so much.' But he didn't go. He couldn't live without me, he said. He was the last of the romantics. He took Billuns's gun and locked himself in the room on Morningside Avenue and shot himself." She paused; she was breathing rapidly, in shallow beats, still fingering that thread. A helicopter was hovering somewhere nearby, its blades dully beating at the air. "I found him," Louise said. "I put him on the bed, I don't know how, he was a big man. Somehow I had to do it, it was important, I don't know why. I sat with him through the entire afternoon. I've never known such silence. And a week later I married Rubin Sinclair." She lifted a hand and laid it over her eyes, as if to shade them against a glare falling from above. "When David was born, I think Rubin knew. He never said anything, but I think he knew. He wasn't a fool. And he was good to me, in his way. He didn't denounce me, didn't demand that Billuns horsewhip me. He plodded on, until everything just quietly fell apart. And then I met you."

"Did your father find out?" Glass said. "About David, I mean, whose son he was?"

"I don't know," she said. "Probably. He knew everything about everything, why not this, too?"

"And you're sure that Varriker killed himself?"

She did not look at him. "I have to be," she said, in almost a whisper, "haven't I? Anything else is unthinkable." Now she lifted her eyes and met his questioning stare. "I know what my father is, but I must believe he isn't that wicked." They sat for a long moment looking at each other. Then she leaned back in the chair and sighed. "I thought it was all over and done with, until that young man phoned the apartment that day."

"It was you he spoke to?"

"Of course — who else?"

"How did *he* know about Varriker and the rest of it?"

"He wouldn't say. There were people I confided in at the time, friends, so-called, I suppose he tracked them down. I don't know. I had to do something, of course. If he had gone to Billuns it would have been the end of everything, the Trust, David's future, everything. I told him I would come and see him. I took the gun. I —"

"Stop," Glass said. "Tell me the truth."

"I *am*. I *am* telling you the truth —" She put a hand quickly into the pocket of her green coat and brought out something compact and darkly a-gleam and set it down on the desk before him. He could read the manufacturer's name clearly on the short, fluted barrel. "There," she said. "There, if you don't believe me!"

He picked up the Beretta and hefted it in his hand. "Where did you get this?" She said nothing. The helicopter was gone, and in its wake the silence in the room had become hollow. He set down the gun between them again. "How did he know?" he asked.

"Who? What?"

"David. How did he know about Riley? Was he there when Riley phoned you?" He made a fist and crashed it down on the desk, making the pistol jump. "*Was he?*" Something came into her face then that he had never seen before: it was the look, dismayed, helpless, lost, that she would have when she was old. She stared at the weapon on the desk and nodded listlessly. She said something, but so quietly he could not hear and had to ask her to say it again. She cleared her throat. "He was right," she said. "We all did it, me, you, all of us. What does it matter who pulled the trigger?"

"It matters, Lou," he said. "Tell me."

She buried her hands in the pockets of her coat and drew in her shoulders, folding herself into herself, as if she were suddenly cold. "Yes," she said, "David was there when Dylan Riley called. He saw how I looked when I heard what Riley had to say. He made me tell him. He said he would go and talk to Riley, that he would reason with him, offer him money, if necessary. I didn't know" — she reached out a hand as if to touch him but faltered and braced her fingers instead on the side of the desk — "I didn't know what he would do. He's so damaged, John. Rubin treated him dreadfully, and then you rejected him — yes, you did, don't deny it! You could have tried. You could have been a father to him."

Her words settled heavily between them, a darker darkness where the lamplight could not reach.

"David knew about Varriker?" Glass asked. She nodded. "When did you tell him?"

"Long ago. I shouldn't have, I suppose. I thought he had the right to know."

"So the bullet through Dylan Riley's eye was a memorial to his father, yes?"

"He's *damaged*, John!"

"And we all did that, too, is that what you're saying?" He looked out at the garish night. "Well, at least now I know," he said, "who the patsy in the room is."

"What?"

"Nothing. Just something someone said to me, once."

She stood up, very slowly, like a person in pain. "I'm going now," she said. "You have to decide what to do. You have your" — she laughed shortly — "your 'story'." She looked at him with compassion, almost. "It's up to you, John," she said. "I'm sorry, but it's up to you."

Also available in ISIS Large Print:

Shafted

Mandasue Heller

Larry Logan is a small-time TV star with a mile-wide ego. Gutted when his latest show is axed, he's less than impressed when the only work he can get is fronting a fake game show — actually an undercover police sting to entrap criminals.

His reluctance evaporates when the show rockets his career back to prime-time stardom. And when lovely, shy Stephanie enters his life, he thinks he finally has it made.

But then it all begins to go wrong. Larry is arrested, on-screen, for a shocking crime. He's shafted some dangerous men — is this their revenge?

ISBN 978-0-7531-8164-5 (hb)
ISBN 978-0-7531-8165-2 (pb)

The Twilight Time

Karen Campbell

Anna Cameron is a new Sergeant in the Flexi unit. On her first day in the new job she discovers she'll be working with her ex, Jamie, now married with a child. In at the deep end emotionally after many years without him, she's also plunged headlong into the underworld of Glasgow's notorious Drag — the haunt of working girls, drug dealers and sad, seedy men. Someone is carving up the faces of local prostitutes, an old man has been brutally killed and racist violence is on the rise. Anna must deal with all this, alongside tensions and backstabbing within her own team.

ISBN 978-0-7531-8072-3 (hb)
ISBN 978-0-7531-8073-0 (pb)

Still Waters

Judith Cutler

DCS Fran Harman has never been happier. Her relationship with Assistant Chief Constable Mark Turner is going well and they are buying a house together. At work, a former protégé, Simon Gates, has just become her new boss.

But Simon's attitude has changed, and Mark's daughter seems hell-bent on destroying their domestic harmony. Even the environment is hostile, the water in Fran's village tainted by something in the local reservoir. Some good old-fashioned detective work seems a useful antidote, even when it's an investigation into something no one really believes is a crime.

Then a dramatic discovery leads to her case becoming a full-blown murder investigation and things come to a head. As the investigation takes its toll on those around her, the waters surrounding her future in the force become increasingly muddy — and possibly threaten her future with Mark.

ISBN 978-0-7531-8024-2 (hb)
ISBN 978-0-7531-8025-9 (pb)

The Silver Swan

Benjamin Black

Time has moved on for Quirke, the world-weary pathologist first encountered in Christine Falls. It is the middle of the 1950s, that low, dishonourable decade; a woman he loved has died, a man whom he once admired is dying, while the daughter he denied for so long is still finding it hard to accept him as her father.

When Billy Hunt, an acquaintance from college days, approaches him about his wife's apparent suicide, Quirke recognises trouble but, as always, trouble is something he cannot resist. Slowly he is drawn into a twilight world of drug addiction, sexual obsession, blackmail and murder, a world in which even the redoubtable Inspector Hackett can offer him few directions.

ISBN 978-0-7531-8118-8 (hb)
ISBN 978-0-7531-8119-5 (pb)